HORRIBLE DISASTERS

from
HorrorAddicts.net

Edited by

Larriane Barnard

Printed in the United States of America.
Edited by Larriane Barnard
Cover art: Thierry Pouzergues
Publisher: HorrorAddicts.net
          Emerian Rich
          David Watson
          HorrorAddicts@gmail.com

ISBN: 978-1463669447

www.horroraddicts.net

HORRIBLE DISASTERS

HORROR ADDICTS CALL TO ARMS
by Emerian Rich

Disaster is the great equalizer. An earthquake doesn't care what race you are, how much you make a year, or what your sexual preference is. We are all at risk.

As the daughter of a minister, my childhood was spent handing out food to disaster survivors while keeping them calm in the church basement as tornados passed overhead. Many of those people we helped had their homes ripped from them in an instant. Some would return to find everything but one wall of their home gone. Others, we helped scavenge the wreckage for any small token or memento that they could grasp onto to make the loss easier. We were cooks, friends, and counselors during a time when they needed a helping hand to pull them through the devastation.

I've helped with tornados, floods, earthquakes, fires, and severe winter storms. The victims are much the same—lost, broken, and in shock. Yet, at no other time is the human spirit so venerable, so true, and I often saw a survivor's soul as they grieved for a home, a pet, or a loved one. It can be surreal and unsettling to lose control of your environment, and it takes a strong spirit to survive. If you've been a disaster relief worker, you've shared in their pain, helped them deal with loss, and coached them to survive. Often, you build long lasting friendships with the ones you work with, almost like soldiers on the battlefield. When you are fighting to save lives, all boundaries go down, and you see how courageous your fellow humans can be.

So please, next time you witness a disaster on the news, don't just watch in awe. Become part of the solution. I encourage you to find ways in your own community to help those who have lost their stability to a natural disaster. Donate time, money, or food. If you don't know where or how to give, contact Rescue Task Force, an organization that has been alleviating suffering and bringing support to disaster victims since 1988. Rescue Task Force goes where others do not, doing what others will not. From the jungles of Central America to the mountains of Kosovo, from tsunami ravaged Thailand to hurricane and fire disaster stricken communities in the United States, their representatives are there, providing immediate disaster relief. By buying this book you have already contributed to the cause, but if you feel you want to do more, go to rescuetaskforce.org. Donating online is quick and easy. Make a onetime donation or chose to give more regularly. Whatever way you decide to help, know that to those who are on the receiving end, your selfless gift is priceless.

Emerian Rich

HorrorAddicts.net Publisher

HORRIBLE DISASTERS

All those involved in this publication have donated their work to benefit disaster relief. Proceeds will be donated to the Rescue Task Force.

Horror authors were given the task of creating a horror story set during a real natural disaster. The horror element had to coincide with the disaster timeline but did not have to be directly involved with the real danger of the event.

The story that started it all, Hammersmith House, was written after Emerian studied the true accounts of survivors of the earthquake and fire that took place in San Francisco in 1906. So moved by their stories, she could not help but write a story in their world. What must it have been like to have friends and family perish in such a disaster? How did they live in the days and weeks afterwards? What mysterious changes might have taken place in their world that no one would notice because of their immediate needs?

The authors of this anthology shall attempt to explore the unexplained. It is up to you, the reader, to decide…was nature truly the cause of such horrors?

2005 YU55
by Garth von Buchholz

He brushed past her, no contact,
each one at arm's length,
yet she could feel the air stream,
feel it from his overcoat
as it billowed; not enough time
under the blue-white streetlights
to catch a look at his face——
no, it was only his power, grace,
that made her turn 90 degrees
and desire him with her tears.

What would this crush have meant to her?
she asked herself,

in the vast, eventless evening,
strolling round that well worn path
while the neighborhood lunatic
stalked her from the shadows,
smiling his admiration,
she fantasized an embrace
to crack mountains, drain oceans,
and pierce her very breast
with the kind of pain that,
to the lonesome and untouched,
is relief from the hollow centuries
of calling out. Calling out,
for the equidistant others to draw closer,
for they never do, never
and such a long never that has been.

As he dashed on,
dissolving into darkness,
her heart burned, would not cool.
She knew not about
the man in the overcoat,
that he was no more than a missile
colder than Neptune,
an assassin of order.

Had he turned a degree
and granted her that embrace,
she would have been raped
by a transient Death,
for whom the amoral act
would become self-destruction,
and no one would know, or care.

Only the madman would be witness.

Garth von Buchholz is an author of poetry, short fiction, non-fiction, and drama. His last book of poetry, *Mad Shadows*, was published in June 2010. His short story, "Make Mad the Roaring Winds," was published in Feb 2012. To find out more about Garth, go to:

vonBuchholz.com

HAMMERSMITH HOUSE
by Emerian Rich
San Francisco Earthquake and Fire, 1906

The following letters were discovered in the hope chest of Mrs. Julia Simons of Montpelier, Vermont following her death in 1972.

WESTERN UNION TELEGRAPH COMPANY
Julia, Earthquake. I am safe. Maddy.

April 20, 1906
My loving sister Julia,

I've written now three short letters to you in haste as various people I knew were going to the postal office. After hearing of even more destruction by earthquake and fire, I hold little hope the letters reached you.

I am assured this letter will find you and will attempt to relate matters as clearly as my muddled memory allows. It has been so very trying on us all. One cannot sleep with all that has gone on.

I can only guess how frightened you must've been hearing the news. What horrible secondhand reports you must've heard. I assure you, your sister is safe.

That is not to say San Francisco is free of devastation. Far from it. It is but two days after the quake and we are still finding our old haunts are in ruins, friends we loved are gone, and our city has been literally "shook" to its core.

As you know, Miss V and I were staying at the place on Jones Street. Both soundly asleep in bed, the whole building began to rock and shudder. Books fell from shelves, knickknacks crashed, and chairs toppled as if we were accosted by a poltergeist. I froze in place, covering my head with a pillow while Miss V ran about the apartment screaming of the second coming!

When it all settled, you could hear a pin drop, it was so serenely quiet. I suppose everyone was just as baffled as we or— and this I did not want to think on— they could not make a sound because they were knocked out by falling objects. Soon sound returned. Voices, screaming, and calling could be heard beyond the great rumble of what I presume were buildings falling to the ground.

Miss V and I dressed in our day clothes and went about the building, collecting those who were not already out. We count ourselves lucky being only afflicted with two minor injuries in our building and none dead.

Shortly after all apartments were cleared. A stout man who just moved in, I think his name to be Sherman, said we might want to grab a suitcase. He thought they might evacuate us because the building to our left leaned into ours.

Good thing Mr. Sherman did suggest this, for we have learned today our place has been burned to the ground.

Do not be sad for us. It was our home for such a short time and most of my jewels are in the bank across town which, thankfully, still stands. As for my beautiful gowns? Much easier replaced compared to having to replace your favorite sister, I think.

Our biggest concern is we only possess two dresses each and none of the shops have reopened yet. I dare say I can manage. Since the curfew is so early, Miss V and I are content with doing a little cleaning up just before dark. Our things are then dry by morning. Curfew is early and no light, not even a candle, is allowed.

Where we have landed is the strangest coincidence of all. Do you remember our distant cousin Reginald? Turns out he was visiting a school friend here in town when the quake occurred. We just happened to see him at the shops a week yesterday, and he seemed quite taken with Miss V.

When the earthquake took us, he rushed to where we were staying to see if we were all right. Moments later, we were walking to his friend's home on Gough Street. Quite a trek, but it was not to be helped. No auto or carriage could have maneuvered through the wreckage and throng of people walking to safe ground.

Now we reside, quite comfortably, I must say, at the Hammersmith residence located just outside the current burn zone. We hope it will continue to be safe. It is strange how the flames stopped just a few streets from us, but they tell me the fire brigade was able to dynamite the fire away. Seems a strange concept, does it not? Perhaps this is what they mean by fighting fire with fire?

More later, as I wish to put this letter in the hand of a servant who is on his way back to his family in Los Angeles. He will attempt to mail it outside of this disaster. It's the only way to be sure you receive it.
Your safe sister,
Maddy

April 22, 1906
Jules,

We've just come from the post empty handed. I have little hope of receiving anything from you for quite some time. Anything sent before the earthquake is most assuredly burned.

Most of the fires have stopped. I hear much of what is going on in different parts of the city and do not wish to frighten you with tall tales of death, destruction, and criminal behavior. I'm sure the circulars are doing nothing to calm your fears. I do assure you, all of this is quite removed from us. As for the damage to the city, although the quake shook us, the fire did even more damage. All the water mains have ruptured, you see, and the fire brigade had no means to help them. The bulk of the fire stopped yesterday, but we all lay in wait for the next flames to rise. The servants of this fine house cook outside as mandated by law. The chimneys appear to be fine, but the owners will not be granted use of them until they are inspected, which I suspect will be many weeks.

I should stop with all the doom and gloom and tell you of our saviors. The lady of the house is Mrs. Eugenia Hammersmith, a widow with one son and one daughter. Mrs. H praises the Lord on high at every turn. Oh, how blessed to have our health! Oh, how fortunate to not be enveloped in flames! These sentiments I cannot agree with more, but the pronunciation of such exclamations for hours on end could drive a person mad.

Her eldest, Mr. Sebastian Hammersmith, is the aforementioned friend of Reginald. He seems to think his mother the stupidest bird this side of the continent. He is not a pleasant man, but seems less grumbly when Mrs. H retires for the afternoon.

I say afternoon, and it is not an exaggeration. Half-past noon, she takes to coughing, her nurse hurries her away, and we do not see her return till breakfast.

Miss V asked Reginald if she retires because the curfew is so early, but he said, no, it has always been with no further explanation.

The third resident of the Hammersmith family is an insufferable woman by the name of Cox. They claim she is the sister of Mrs. H, though I can see no similarity. Where Mrs. H is all heaven and praise God, Mrs. Cox is fire and brimstone. They tell me Mrs. H will not be in the same room as her sister. I assume it is for this reason I see little of her.

Young Mr. Hammersmith regards the women with equal disdain. In fact, the only time he utters more than a groan is when they are absent. We asked Reginald why he would befriend such a stoic figure as Mr. H. His response humored us.

"There's a certain peace in having an acquaintance I don't have to entertain the whole day," said he. "Sebastian is the same whether at home or about town. So, there's no need to plan a thing."

Miss V and I have been stowed away in the coziest room, the bedroom of Miss Beth, Mrs. H's daughter. She is abroad and will not return until late October, by which time I hope to have Miss V settled at school and be comfortably back home with you in Montpelier.

In the meantime, Mrs. H bid us use whatever we may need from Miss Beth's wardrobe. Miss V took offense at first, but I reminded her, we've been wearing the same garments for five days. I welcome the thought of fresh clothes, though we still aren't afforded a proper bath.

And so there you have it, dear sister. I am safe and well despite living in a home of adversaries.

We are about to walk to see if we can find a post office open to send this. Hope all is well with the family there.

Your devoted sister,

Maddy

April 25, 1906

Beloved Sister,

Yesterday I received your six letters, one from before the earthquake, to my surprise, and five since.

I am truly sorry to have brought you such worry on those first days, but I am glad Mr. Sherman succeeded in his task of placing the telegram so you could receive it as soon as possible.

I understand father's wish for me to return home. However, I've come to set Miss V up at school, and I plan to do it. She needs me now, more than ever. I am happy to report though many schools have suffered badly, hers had only minor damage. They hope to reopen at the end of May. Then I shall be heading home to you all. What a merry reunion we shall have! I'm afraid my gifts burned, but perhaps I can get some more before I leave.

We are getting along here at Hammersmith House with little inconvenience. The gentlemen are obliged to help with street cleanup for several hours every day. Though perhaps men of luxury most of their lives, they do not seem to mind the labor and return with stories to tell.

As for Miss V and I, we have been helping with the house duties the servants can't seem to get to. Cooking outside the house takes much longer.

I know you have never seen your sister work so hard in her life. When we are not working, we've taken up knitting little things for the children of the families who have lost their homes and camp out in the park. With my knack for the pastime, you can be assured they are very little things. I stick to baby booties. I've made fifteen in all. Miss V is better skilled than I and has made over forty things. Those poor children in the park, Sister. If you saw them, you would do the same. Where will they go?

Our lives are not all work. We are able to walk, though it is a fair distance, to the post every other day before curfew.

Mr. H and Reginald often join us, they say for our protection, but we suspect they wish to be out as much as we. We are all suffering a bit of cabin fever with the city in shambles and events not going on as usual. I suspect another reason for Reginald escorting us is to see more of Miss V. They walk closer every day.

Miss V would do well to make a match with Reginald, and it would make his mother sigh relief as he is approaching forty with no lady to call his own.

Whilst Miss V spends time with her "Reggie" as she now lovingly calls him, I am often left in the company of Mr. H, whose disposition grows on me. He is quiet and unenthusiastic about much, but like R said, I find company with him very relaxing as if he's not even there. He reads as I knit. He walks in silence next to me as the others fall behind and I compile shopping lists in my head.

Oh! I forgot to tell you, and you would do well to keep this from father, I found a secret chamber. I was in the Hammersmith's library and tugged on a book by Shelley which would not come loose. Suddenly a section of the bookcase moved, and to my surprise, a draft of cool air licked at my ankles.

You know your sister too well to not guess what happened next. I went in tentatively. The passage was dark, and it took my eyes a bit to adjust. The dust and cobwebs were thick, but mostly around the edges, telling me even though the place was never cleaned, someone had been through there recently. The thin hall led to another and another, till I wasn't sure which way was north. At length, I came to a small cluttered room with what appeared to be scientific

17

equipment. Multicolored bottles and beakers made me think it a working lab of some sort. There was a thick tome open on the workspace filled with hardly decipherable notes. Though I wanted to explore, a noise alerted me to the presence of another, and I scurried back down the dusty hall like a rodent running from a house cat. Just before I reentered what I thought to be the library, I felt a pin prick on my neck. As I reached up to discover the cause, a spider the likes I've never seen skittered down my arm. His back was blue-green iridescent, like a peacock feather. His belly was bright sapphire, shining as if it were a jewel. I squealed despite myself, making him jump down to the dusty floor and away. Running to the door before me, I found myself in the conservatory.

The bite on my neck is rather itchy as most bites are, but I have not given in to convulsions or fever. Were doctors plentiful, I would call on one, but they are all tending to the seriously injured. Complaining of a spider bite hardly seems right. Besides being a bit tired from hard work, I feel fine. I plan to take an early night and wake fresh tomorrow.

But a question, sister, who shall I ask about the secret lab? I must get another look at the book! I know you will say curiosity killed the cat, but I must know more!

Your loving sister,
Maddy

April 28, 1906
Jules,

I am writing you from a sick bed. Do not worry, I am not ill. It has been mandated by the gentleman of the house, Mr. H. You must be laughing because you know how much I detest being put to bed, but

Mr. H has commanded I must rest, and Reginald seconded the notion. Beside it being rude were I not to follow house rules, Mrs. H went into fits when I said I would not.

So to bed with me it was, and I am not even allowed to walk to the new shop opening near us today. Reginald is to escort Miss V and even Mrs. H, who never leaves the house, will see the shop before I.

What caused this chain of events is entirely my own doing. I was innocently investigating the aforementioned secret passageway and read a full page of the messy script before I heard a creak in the hall. I stowed the notes I took in my skirts and managed to find the library door. When I exited, Mrs. H was standing there and drew in a great breath.

"Good heavens!" said she. "Why have you come from the bowels of the house?"

You know I love to scavenge, but rarely think of the consequences. I began to address Mrs. H, but felt light-headed and stumbled forward as if to fall.

Mr. H was at my side, appearing as if from nowhere, and spoke to his mother. "The earthquake must've knocked this sealed passageway loose. Who knew we had such a place? Miss Allan, are you quite well? You appear about to faint. Won't you take this seat here?"

I jest you not; my jaw dropped. Never had I seen or heard Mr. H so accommodating. Soon the whole house was in the library. Miss V and Reginald rushed in calling for my safety. Mrs. H was in hysterics for my health, and the servants scurried in and out, taking orders from Mr. H. Mr. H saw me to my room, accompanied by Miss V.

Now I am finally on my own and can write to my sister. This missive must be quickly closed however, for they are to leave within the hour, and I wish them to drop it in the post for me. I still maintain I am well enough to go, but with all my nursemaids, I can't hope to succeed.

Effectively trapped,

Maddy

May 3, 1906

Jules,

Please pardon the messy hand I now write in. I am not in the best of health.

As you know from my last letter, I was sequestered in my room because of a fainting spell. They did not let me go with them to the shop, but it was for the best. Shortly after they left, I began to feel dizzy. I called for the servant. It was not she, but Mr. H who appeared. He apologized, saying the servants were out attending to chores and did I need anything?

How strange to tell him I felt dizzy after my denying of such an event earlier, but truly, I was not well. His look was so kind, so sympathetic; I hardly knew what to do. The dilemma was soon sorted out because I fainted.

When I think of him tending to me and how I must've looked, I am embarrassed. I guess I was out for days. They say I only woke to drink and then took to sleeping again. They tell me a fever took me, and Mr. H would allow no one to enter the room save him and the doctor. Since the earthquake and water supply damage, there has been a great fear of illness being spread, but for Mr. H to endanger himself this way, what was he thinking?

The fever has gone now, but I remain weak. It would appear I am through the worst of it.

I am still baffled by Mr. H's concern. I don't know how to repay such a courtesy. No, I am not in love with him. I am, however, perplexed. Why should such an indifferent fellow be moved to help a stranger such as I?

Maddy

May 8, 1906
Jules,

The city is bouncing back, as am I. Yesterday I was able to take a short walk to the new shop. When I say shop, I should say house, for that is what it is. It feels strange to be purchasing undergarments in someone's dining room, but the saleswoman was pleasant and made me feel at ease.

After a mere thirty minutes outside of the house, I was ready to head back. I sat in the parlor while Miss V and R continued to the post.

Mr. H sat with me and spoke in a voice he obviously did not want others to hear. "What did you find in the chamber?" When I did not respond, he took my trembling hand in his. "I wish you no harm. I know you were in Aunt's chamber, and I only wish to know what you touched."

I could not lie. I told him I saw the book and made some notes. Not until then did I realize I'd lost the notes. They had been in my skirt, but I had forgotten about them.

"Don't worry yourself," said he. "Your notes are safe in your box on the dresser."

I could only be mortified, dear sister. If he'd placed the notes in my box, he would've seen the photo of me and Jackson. He would've noticed the ring box and perhaps read the letter beneath.

My face must've shown my shock, for he gripped my hand tighter and said, "I did not disturb any of your treasures, I assure you."

Tears came, I could not stop them. I suppose I hadn't realized how much of my pain I'd let collect in the box. Mr. H called for a servant to help me up the stairs.

I slept deep and only woke just now. It is morning. I shall stay here for the day if they will allow it.

Love to father and mother and of course to you my loving sister,
Maddy

May 9, 1906
Jules,

Morning and I feel wonderful. How strange it is. I wake early and feel fine, but by midday I wear myself out. The doctor says it might take a while to rebuild my strength, but he has great faith in my full recovery.

The previous part of this letter was written earlier. I've just had the strangest interlude with Mr. H. He knocked on my door as I wrote you. When he entered, he shut the door behind him. I wasn't properly dressed and pulled the covers closer. He asked how I was, and we exchanged pleasantries, but then silence.

He pulled a chair closer to the bed and whispered in a secretive voice, "Miss Allan, I am sorry to have caused you distress the other day, but I must know what happened in the laboratory."

I told him the same thing I had before. I only took notes.

"Nothing else?" he asked me.

I assured him, all the notes I had, he found.

"But, what do the notes mean?" I asked him. "I can find no rhyme or reason to them."

He opened his mouth to speak, but no words came. He remained close, studying me, perhaps wondering if to believe me. With him close to me, I admired his eyes. I never knew they were so blue. Nor had I realized he is a nice looking fellow.

He leaned closer, kissing me on the lips. I tell you, my heart was racing terribly. Even with Jackson my heart did not beat as hard.

When he pulled away, he seemed embarrassed and made to leave. Before I knew what I was about, I grabbed his wrist to stop him. He winced, and I looked down at his hand. A black and blue crescent-shaped bruise colored the flesh between his thumb and finger. Two sore holes were in the center.

"I'm sorry," I said. "I didn't mean to hurt you."

"It's nothing," said he and covered his hand with his jacket sleeve.

"You've been bitten by one of those curious spiders as well? Do you know where they come from?" I asked.

"Pardon me? Spiders? What are you talking about?" His face was a pinch of confusion as he waited for my answer.

I explained about the creature that had bitten me in the secret passageway and showed him my neck. He seemed to register what I said, but I could not guess at his thoughts, his face remained a façade of control.

"I must go," he said. "Sleep well."

As he shut the door, I glanced at my little pocket watch. It was eleven-thirty. Does he know my sleep schedule so well as to know I will fade within the hour?

I wish I had my Jules here to advise me what to do.

Love,

Maddy

May 10, 1906

Jules,

What a difference a day makes. I never completely understood what the phrase meant until recently. Like the city falling overnight, my faith in Mr. H has crashed to ruins. He is a madman or a liar. I know not which.

Yet, he is the reason I rose this morning and dressed to have breakfast with the rest of the household. As I walked down the stairs, I thought fondly of our kiss and touched my lips where his had been.

As I entered the breakfast room, all eyes were on me. It was the first time Mrs. H spoke to me since the library incident. She said I looked very well as did Miss V and Reginald.

Mr. H kept his gaze down and only grunted something I thought was a yes when his mother asked if he thought I looked improved.

During breakfast, I tried to catch his attention, but Mr. H seemed determined to study his plate as if it held the answers to the universe. I assure you it did not! Eggs and cakes can no more tell the future than the next culinary creation.

After breakfast, we filed out. I followed Mr. H, catching his arm, careful not to touch his bruised hand.

"Mr. Hammersmith," I said and then a little quieter I shyly called his first name. "Sebastian."

When he heard me use his Christian name, he looked into my eyes, and I thought I might melt.

That's when I noticed the entire right side of his face was bruised. I reached up to touch it, but he motioned to escort me outside. He led me into the garden to a shaded area where a once great tree laid on its side.

In the daylight, I could see his bruise much better. It looked frightfully painful. As I was about to ask what had caused it, he took me in his arms and kissed me. I thought I must be in heaven. We smiled a secret smile only those in love can share.

"What's happened to you, love?" I asked. I could not have guessed what he said next, yet I remember it so clearly.

He said, "You want to know whose bruise this is? It is yours. You caused it last night."

I knew he was insane. I had been sleeping since noon the previous day.

"I know it's hard to believe, dear. The spider that bit you has caused a certain 'change' in you. A rift, if you will. When you sleep, you rise as another being. A mean being, who wishes to harm others. I have been tending to you at night, feeding you, but last night things turned..." He looked at me, and I could do nothing but stare.

"You lashed out, knocked me down, and I could not follow. You only returned to your bed early this morning. I know not where you went, but when you returned, there was blood on your dress and in your hair. I was so concerned for you."

He placed a hand on my cheek, true worry showing in his eyes, though as you can imagine, I was taken aback by his statements. How could he make up such lies and believe them so adamantly?

"My mother was bitten years ago. She is now a conflicted being as you are. She stays mostly in her lab, trying to find a cure."

25

"Her lab? I thought it was your aunt's?"

He swallowed, taking a deep breath before answering. "My mother and aunt are one in the same. It is easier to tell visitors they are but sisters, for who would believe the truth?"

"Yet you're expecting me to believe it?"

He squeezed my hand and pulled me close.

"You will learn," said he. "To control it as mother has. But for now, we must leave town. There is a place we own, in the mountains. You will be safe there. I can take care of you. I only wish I had been able to protect you from this. I ask your forgiveness for being bitten in my house."

"But you were bitten too! Yet you did not get the fever or become this monstrosity you claim I've become."

"This?" he asked, holding up his hand. "This is not a spider's bite. It's yours, my love."

I ran from him. Ran here to write you. He thankfully has not followed.

What can be his purpose for making up such lies? For taking advantage of a woman recovering from fever? I am so disturbed, I feel ill. To be jilted in love in such a way! I must retire. First thing tomorrow, I will seek transport back home.

Your heart-broken sister,

Maddy

May 11, 1906

My dear, dear Julia,

This is the hardest letter I've ever penned.

I love you most in the world, and yet I must tell you, I may never see you again, at least not for many years. Please give father and mother my love. I don't know what you are to tell them, and I am sorry for giving you this burden to bear. You certainly can't tell them the truth. Nor can I tell you the whole of it.

I can only say I have wronged Sebastian. I did call him crazy as would anyone in my position, but now I know he is right.

This morning I woke in a place I've never been, wearing a frock which is not mine, with someone I've never seen.

Thank heaven for Bast. He is a pillar of strength and he loves me—all of me.

We now travel to his family's mountain house, I know not where. I cannot, for your safety, give the new address.

I love you, my dear sister, my closest friend. It pains me to know you will lose me. My heart aches when I think I will not see your children grow. Perhaps in a few years—. No, I must not think on this. We must not hold out hope. Just promise me you will remember the good times when we were happy together.

As we left San Francisco today, I saw the extent of the devastation the earthquake and fire made. And then we saw, from a high hill, the unharmed portion, solid and pristine. I relate it to myself.

During this trial not only the earth split, but my soul cracked. There is a part of me just outside the burn zone—fresh, whole, clean, and then there is the other side, the hidden side, even I do not see, one burnt and ugly. Only Sebastian carries the burden of knowing my evil. Oh God! He does truly love me, but what a task to ask of a mere mortal man.

I can only hope when we return to this broken city, it is mended as I hope to be.

I love you, sister, with all my heart. Please take care of yourself.

Your broken sister, Maddy

Emerian Rich is a writer, artist, and Horror Hostess of the popular international podcast, <u>HorrorAddicts.net</u>. She is best known for her *Night's Knights Vampire Series*. She also writes the *Sweet Dreams Musical Romance Series* under the name Emmy Z. Madrigal. For more information, go to:

<u>emzbox.com</u>

MAWGAWR AT BOSCASTLE
by Ed Pope
Boscastle Flood, 2004

Sometime around midday on the 16th of August 2004, a pitch black cloud materialised overhead. Unbeknownst to the people of Boscastle and the many tourists visiting the beautiful Cornish fishing village, Hurricane Alex swirled in the Atlantic, forming a dark mass of rain clouds seven miles high over the mainland. A vast black ocean hung in the air, waiting to fall earthwards.

Jim walked to the village pub. England was playing the West Indies in cricket, and he had just enough time for a pint and to catch some of the Test Match before he had to pick his wife up from the hairdressers. He hurried as the sky began to bruise darker still, making it seem like night was falling early. This effect was made even starker by the high granite cliffs forming the river valley in which the village lay. Looking downstream and out to sea, Jim saw a weather front so foreboding it gladdened his heart to be approaching the warmth and comfort of the pub's glowing interior.

"Afternoon, Bill."

"Afternoon," replied Bill. The smiling landlord reached for a handled pint glass in anticipation of his order. "And what an afternoon it is."

"You're not wrong there. Still, at least, they're not rained off at Old Trafford," said Jim nodding towards the game on the television.

"No, and we're not doing too badly either for a change. Pint of Best, is it?"

"Better make it a shandy. I've got to pick Hannah up in a bit."

"Right you are then."

Bill pulled the pint, and Jim looked at the large TV screen as England's cricketers approached one-hundred runs.

"Two pounds eighty, please," said Bill and placed the drink on the bar.

As Jim handed over the money an ear-splitting crash from outside shook the room. The sound seemed to come from all directions. Everyone in the pub fell silent and collectively held their breath. A few seconds later the water fell. Not rain as such, as that implies droplets. Sheets of water fell from the sky. Within seconds the level of the river, visible from the bay windows in the pub, rose by a couple of feet in a chocolate-brown and foaming torrent.

"What the..." cried one of the drinkers in the pub.

Everyone turned to look. The view up the valley was partially obscured by the hammering rain, but all the drinkers could clearly see the surreal image of a six-foot wave thundering down the small river towards the village, bursting the riverbanks as it came.

Within seconds the valley was flooding, the river channel no longer visible, and the swirling mass of raging water covered the streets. Within minutes the water came into the pub.

Some of the onlookers in the bar, who had previously been shocked into silence, started to shriek as the first cars washed out to sea, as if what had previously been a river was now a perverse highway.

"Hannah!" Almost oblivious to how he had vocalised the thought of the danger his wife could be in, he turned for the door, swung it open, and stepped out into a hellish waterscape where only minutes previously his village had been.

His first instinct was to get in his car, but the roads were already under water and parked cars were dislodging and slipping away. As if to add an exclamation point, a tree washed down the road past him.

"Shit," he said out loud.

Jim realised if he was going to get to Hannah, it would be on foot. Struggling against the rising surge of brown floodwater already at knee level, he clung to the sides of buildings until he came to the river bridge. With no time for a second thought he charged over it.

As he did, a terrifying sound like a sledgehammer meeting rock caused him to turn. The stone of the bridge caved in and a wall of furious water and masonry hit him in the chest.

Winded and unbalanced, the barrage of water pushed him to the other side of the bridge and toppled him head-first into the roaring chasm below. Like landing on a moving train, the terrifying sense of disorientation under the surface was nothing compared to the dawning reality of his situation as he pulled his head clear of the water to gasp in vital air.

The bridge he had been thrown from was rapidly disappearing into the distance such was the speed of the water carrying him off. His legs and body were battered by underwater objects, rocks and trees transported as if they weighed no more than sediment.

Jim's foot caught on an obstruction, dragging him under like a fishing float. A log hurtling in the current smashed into his backside sending searing pain up his spine, but mercifully knocking him free, saving him, perhaps only temporarily, from drowning as a piece of flotsam.

Jim tried to swim across the current to avoid being swept out to sea. Very quickly he realised that was impossible. Even if he could power through the rampant water, dodging the increasing amount of logs and cars would be equally unfeasible. In a strange moment of absolute clarity, which he surmised was only attainable when fighting for one's life, Jim resolved to allow the current to take him to sea and save his energy reserves for the battle surely lying ahead.

He did not have to wait long. The current of the floodwater pushed his battered body out of what was left of the harbour and beyond the rocky outcrops of the cove in which the village was situated. In the distance, Jim could see the extent of the worsening devastation. Buildings subsided, and dozens of cars stormed downstream, taking the same journey he just had. Despite the severity of his current predicament, Jim momentarily felt lucky to be alive.

The waves in the open sea lifted and tossed him, and the wind bit at his exposed head. In a strange way being stranded at sea felt comforting compared to being caught in the floodwaters.

Jim had grown up there, and like most men from those parts he was a lifelong swimmer, surfer, and fisherman. He knew the sea and the local coastline, most of which was sheer cliffs with the occasional bay. In no way would he be able to swim back against the flow to Boscastle. He would have to swim a mile or so to a nearby cove where, hopefully, he'd be able to get ashore.

Heading west, he started a steady swim. Focusing on an irregular rhythm, he allowed the waves to lift him up to power through his strokes to swim down them. Every few minutes he would get swept under the water, but he always managed to reach the surface and restart his progress.

Every time his spirits dropped, he was grateful for his escape from the floodwaters while he feared for Hannah and his other friends in the village. How many people were dead, and how many people had lost their homes? Had he lost his home? Did he have anything left worth swimming for?

Pushing such dark thoughts out of his mind, Jim stopped to tread water for a moment and assess his progress. He travelled west, parallel to the coast, at a reasonable rate, but the tide and currents took him inland much quicker than he hoped. He feared being taken too close to the rock walls of the cliffs and being battered against them before he could reach the cove, a prospect more than likely unavoidable. With no other option, he carried on swimming.

The monotony of the battle to traverse through the waves allowed for the first time the pain of his ordeal to seep through. The salt water stung the cuts and lacerations on his body, and his ribs and muscles ached deeply from the various impacts they had suffered. His arms and legs tired, and the unwelcome burn of exhaustion spread.

A large wave threw him out of the water, and as he gathered his composure he saw he was only about fifty feet from the cliffs. Meeting the dark, sharp rocks was now going to be inevitable. The alternative to not attempt to swim along the edges of the ominous rock face against the tide was a certain drowning.

As Jim was about to resume his front crawl, the velvety sensation caused by a swell of displaced water below him infused over his body. He paused his strokes and froze motionless in the salty water.

What the hell was that? It could have been a dolphin, a seal, possibly a harmless basking shark, summer visitors to Cornwall. Perhaps it was just a freak current? Either way, Jim reasoned nothing was to be gained from staying put.

He leant forward to throw his tired arms into a crawl, when his whole body jolted to halt at the sight of a long dark shape gliding underwater along the edge of the approaching cliffs. He gasped, choking on the sour salt water and coughed maniacally. Fuck, fuck—what the fuck was that!

Panic set in. He splashed uncontrollably as he fought to stay afloat in the waves.

The dark figure he had seen was no longer visible. He had definitely seen it though, and it was about forty feet long!

"Basking shark," he said out loud. "Calm the fuck down, it was only a basking shark."

The water between him and the rocks started to roll and swell. Something large moved under the surface. In the middle of the swell a thick tail tapered to a narrow end flicked up into the air and then submerged leaving the water flat behind.

Sheer terror and panic set in.

Jim was already dangerously close to hyperthermia. His skin crawled, and the pores of his skin contracted like that of some grotesque amphibian. He was in the sea with a large creature, the likes of which he had never seen before in those or any other waters.

His legs and feet felt like they were dangling over the entrance to hell. The sense of being exposed to something unknown, in its element and completely at its mercy, tipped his mind over the knife-edge of sanity he had been battling since first washing into the water. He plunged his face under the water;

convinced it would be better to see *something* than to constantly fear what was potentially just underneath his toes.

He saw nothing, and thrust his head—panic stricken—above the undulating waves of the surface. The waves raised him up. He saw nothing.

He descended back into the trough caused by the surrounding surf.

The next wave lifted him up again, all his senses were wired and alert.

He bobbed back down, adrenaline frying his mind with what might lurk below.

The next wave lifted him above the surrounding water and revealed a hideous face, part canine, part serpentine, on the end of a long neck, raised six foot out of the water. As the wave brought Jim back down again the creature turned its head and looked at him.

The descending wave obscured it from view.

"Mawgawr!" screamed Jim's mind.

Like most areas near lakes or seas there were old stories of water monsters, denizens of the mysterious underwater world. The local one had the old Cornish name of Mawgawr. The memory of seeing its face and being in the water with it kicked Jim's flight-or-fight response into action. He swam like a man possessed.

Jim didn't see the barrel-like wake heading towards him until after he had felt it. It started to drag him backwards and down into the water. The displaced water, and the terrifying shape underneath, travelled beyond Jim's body. Dreading what would happen next, and utterly deranged with fear, Jim watched as the wake decreased. The animal submerged into the depths. In an instant, Jim was alone on top of the water, but not in it.

He could almost see the cove representing his exit from the trauma, but he would be in the water at least another hour, possibly more if the conditions worsened. He couldn't tolerate being at the mercy of what lay beneath the surface for another second. The current pushed him towards the rocky cliff face. He resolved to work with it. Perhaps he could find a handhold and pull himself out of the water?

Rescue boats and helicopters would surely start patrolling at some point, and hanging on to a freezing cliff all night would be better than staying in the water.

He threw himself into a ferocious pace, swimming to the rocks which had previously represented his greatest fear but then looked like salvation. With every thrust of his legs, he dreaded the sensation of feeling them meet something solid and monstrous.

The water around the rocks rose and fell dangerously, waves crashed against them in an explosion of white water. Again and again Jim's body was thrown at the rock and sliced on the jagged, barnacle encrusted stone.

He reached for a handhold. A wave gathered him up and threw him into the wall of rock, breaking his nose. Blood streamed from his mouth and nostrils, making breathing even more difficult.

Again he was lifted skyward by the pounding waters. He reached out and grabbed on to the rock. For a tantalising moment he dangled from the dark stone barricade, legs scrabbling for purchase. The surface of the rock was like ice in both temperature and texture. Jim fell backwards into the throbbing surf.

Floating on his back, half-dazed, half-drowned, his view skywards was obscured by an evil grin, widening and growing ever larger as it screamed closer to him. The watery bed on which he lay started to drop away beneath him. Yet *that mouth* got closer and closer, bigger and bigger, until everything went black.

Ed Pope's love of horror spans from Victorian ghost stories to the most modern extreme cinema and literature. More accustomed to writing non-fiction on the genre, he is known as the author of "Transgressive Cinema" and has contributed to "Exquisite Terror." Ed has been the voice of the European horror scene on HorrorAddicts.net and is a staff writer. To find out more about Ed, go to:

TransgressiveCinema.com

ASHFALL
by Mark Eller
Mount Vesuvius Volcanic Eruption, 79 A.D.

"God will save us, Atlus," Julia promised as my master gave an upward thrust to an impossibly thin sword, driving it deep into Luccia's lower belly. Luccia gasped, and hot metal sizzled as the sword's tip broke between her shoulder blades. Steaming blood created a stench almost lost inside the smoke-shrouded smithy. The pounding clang of apprentice driven hammers drowned out her cries, but even when weeping, her open eyes remained steady on the worthless icon clenched in her fist.

When Luccia died, her hand relaxed. The icon fell, and her young head tilted forward. Vul jerked the sword free, and Luccia fell to the floor where her body lay near half a dozen others. Vul's wolf-sized lizard, Erius, lifted its head from where it fed on Scipio's body, scuttled to Luccia, and sank its teeth into her naked thigh.

"Ha!" Vul half-shouted, stamping his foot. Beneath us, the earth trembled. Turning, he studied me with dark eyes sunk deep into a twisted visage. "Another life lost, one you thought to save. Kill this last blasphemer, Atlus. Embolden my masterpiece with a second soul, one taken by your mortal hands, and I will let you live."

The chain attached to my left wrist, fastened by an iron staple to a thick oak beam, rattled as I fought the urge to lunge toward him. Though short, my master stood heavy and unnaturally strong. Every life he stole added to his power. Here in Pompeii, he inspired fear beyond reason.

Julia watched me with steady eyes. Her face appeared plain and haggard. Her thin body, as naked as mine, was ravaged by the diseases of her forced trade. Her belly and thighs showed angry scars; her breasts, flaccid from nursing, hung low. Nestled between them, on a leather cord, hung an icon similar to Luccia's. Stroking the icon with one finger, she fastened her strong, dark eyes on mine. Only moments from dying, Julia looked at me with more strength and courage than had many of the gladiators I had faced in the arena.

"Preserve yourself," she begged. "Kill me."

Weak from both hunger and my whip-torn back, I looked into Vul's crow-cruel eyes while fear churned in my guts.

"Redeem yourself," Vul encouraged. Firelight reflected against his dark orbs as Erius ripped Luccia's flesh free. "Come back to me, Atlus."

Lips thinning, Julia nodded, telling me, "You should have murdered us in the arena. We didn't expect to live."

"I kill warriors and thieves," I told my master. "Not blasphemers. I will not murder her soul."

Cursing, Vul spun away, pulled a thick-bladed sword from a forge-oven, and turned back, holding the glowing red steel in an unprotected grip. Two limping steps brought him to Julia. Grasping her ragged hair with his free hand, he forced her to look down on him.

"And what about you? Same offer I gave the others. Renounce your blasphemy. Prove you accept the true gods by quenching this sword inside Atlus's belly, and you shall live. This blade already tasted Scipio. Give it one more soul and I'll set you free."

Julia paled, but her courage held. "My god protects me."

"Like he protected them?" Vul roared, and once again the earth shook. He waved a hand toward the bodies. "My friend feeds well."

"My god protects me," Julia repeated.

"Whore!" my master spat, drawing back his sword hand.

I lunged. The chain pulled me back, but not before Vul flinched.

A low chuckle filled the air, one that seemed amused by Vul's momentary fear. At its sound the apprentice's hammering stilled, and the forge fires died.

"Have you fallen so far, brother?" a man's voice asked from the doorway.

Looking up from its meal, the lizard hissed as the man moved into view. My already tight belly clenched tighter. Where Vul stood short and crippled, this man was tall, clean, and solid. He possessed hard features above an even harder body. An ivory grin formed beneath steel eyes. At his side waited a waist-high beast owning saber fangs and fur blacker than anything I had ever before seen.

"Blood crow! Stealer of wives!" Vul shouted, pointing with the glowing sword. "Be gone from my forge. Be gone from my city. Be gone from my country!"

The intruder stepped deeper into the building, the beast at his side. "Master Smith, creator of wonders, and you can't even convert this whore to your worship at sword point?" He laughed mockingly. "Forget your wife. She's dead. They're all dead but for you and me. I need weapons, brother, weapons that will break walls and destroy souls. Weapons equal to the one you hold in your hand. Give me those and my men will kill so many we'll once again be gods."

41

"Interfering bastard!" Vul cursed. He looked at his cooling sword. "Eight months went into this blade's making." He pointed its tip at Julia, and then at me. "This sword drank in a small part of their essence during its first quenching. The second must happen while it's held in one of their mortal hands. Within moments one shall drive it into the other's belly, and your last hope of dominating me will be gone."

"Eight months in the making and requiring mortal hands?" The man gestured impatiently. "I remember when two minutes would have sufficed. Help me and I will give you back your strength. A thousand swords, Brother. Nay, ten thousand, each imbued with a mortal's soul. I've men waiting, giving me worship and strength. With my army and your weapons, we will rampage and murder and create such fear the mortals will have no choice but to throw the usurper aside and follow us again. It will be like old times except you will be will my artificer instead of Father's."

"I would be your slave," Vul said in a quiet voice.

Around us, the apprentices and slaves slipped away. The stranger's beast drooled, and Erius cracked Luccia's thighbone.

"Better to serve in hell than to be a gnat on Rome's ass," the man snapped. "I've no patience for your quibbling. You will serve me, but all others will lie beneath you."

"You have mocked me," Vul said quietly. "You have broken my limbs and stolen my wife. I will know true death before helping you."

"Serve or die," the man warned. "I may be diminished, but you are nearly drained. You have few believers while I own the faith of ten thousand soldiers. You are almost powerless. Almost worthless."

"Worthless!" Vul stamped his foot, and the earth trembled. "Powerless! I control more than you know. I control a salamander!" He pointed at the lizard. "Erius."

Standing, Erius faced the open doorway. Jaws gaping, strips of raw flesh clung to its teeth. In answer, the man's beast flexed, flowed, grew two new necks and two new heads.

Crippling fear shot into my gut, stronger than ever before. Julia shuddered, and the earth rumbled while outside a sound greater than Zeus' thunder cracked the air. The ground jumped like a wild stallion after being speared. My knees trembled, and the raw lash stripes across my back burned.

Erius released a low hiss. Vapor drifted from its mouth, and then a stream of fire seeming hot enough to cut through iron spurted toward the doorway.

"Vulcan!" the man cursed as he and his beast both dodged to the side. "You'll die for this!"

"Not before you die!" Vulcan shouted, and the earth leaped to another crack of thunder. "I'll not be held beneath the sway of treacherous Mars!"

"Then it is war!" Mars yelled as he leapt outside, laughing. "By week's end this world will own but one god, and it will be me."

Around us, timbers cracked as fire engulfed the building. Heat drove into me like a fist from hell, searing my eyes and lungs, making me jerk back. Over and over, the chain ripped into my wrist, sinking into my flesh as thick smoke stole my breath.

The chain's staple held, but bones within my blood-slick hand broke, crumpled, allowing me to slip free. Outside, Mars roared. A burst of twisted force cracked past the doorway, crashing into Vulcan, driving the sword from his hand. Throwing himself to the floor, he scrabbled about like a broken crab, his hands frantically sweeping across the smoke shrouded floor, muttering. "I'll kill him with a double-souled sword."

"Run, Atlus!" Julia cried.

Without thinking, I leaped through the flames, grabbed a hammer from an anvil, and hurried back to Julia. Half a dozen quick blows broke her chain while embers fell from above, searing into my skin. Once she was free, we ran as Vulcan rose with a triumphant cry, the hilt-less and still glowing sword gripped in his hand.

"Erius!" Vulcan shouted. "Bring back the whore and my slave. I need one of their souls!"

Beneath us, the earth shook once more.

Outside the smithy, the city of Pompeii seemed strangely empty and yet confused. Dozens of people pushed carts or carried packs along the main street. Shop shutters and doors hung open and unattended. Ignoring everything but flight, we ran ten minutes before daring to slow.

I grabbed a slave's arm as she pushed her master's cart. She tried to jerk free, but failed. Even in my weakened state, I remained a gladiator while she was but a woman.

"Tell me where everybody is going and I won't harm you!" I shouted at the slave's master.

Jerking out a short sword, the old man tried a swing so clumsy I had no trouble taking it from him with my broken hand. Within moments I held the blade to his throat, clenched in an embarrassingly weak grip.

"Tell me."

"To the harbor," he whispered, "or one of the gates. We have to leave."

"Why?"

"The mountain. Vesuvius," the slave answered in her master's stead. She gestured behind my shoulder. "It's smoking."

A quick look proved she did not lie. Thick, grey smoke rose in a high spire from the mountain, spreading out at the edges like a tree's branches.

Releasing the slave's arm, I dropped the sword from her master's neck.

"We have to leave," I told Julia, not knowing why I still protected her. An aging whore, her body was unappealing and her demeanor improperly proud and defiant, attributes I found unbecoming in a whore. Perhaps I protected her because we were two slaves on the run or perhaps because she was the last one living of those I had refused to murder. Warrior born and gladiator trained, honor demanded those I kill be wicked or a worthy opponent. When facing Julia and her friends in the arena, I thought them only weak-willed fools who followed a dead god.

Fools maybe, but Julia had since proved they were anything but weak-willed.

Julia grabbed a tunic from the cart, pulled it on, and passed me a cloth for my loins. Taking it, I kicked the old man away, clumsily tied the cloth about my waist with Julia's help, and looked at the sword I still held in my bleeding hand. It bore Vul's maker's mark, another god-cursed soul-quenched blade.

"My sword," the old man protested.

"Is mine," I answered. "Run before I shove it through your heart."

He ran, badly, leaving his slave and cart behind.

"The harbor will be crowded with no boats available," Julia said. "We must go by land."

The old man's slave cursed. Around us, men and women swatted at their heads and arms as dust spouted up from the street. Something struck my neck, and then a blow dug into my whip ravished back. I jerked my head around, searching for shelter.

Bending down, Julia lifted something from the street. Stretching out her arm, she showed me a grey, pitted stone. "Rocks! The sky is breaking."

A screaming woman fell to the road. Blood marred the side of her face. Other stones fell as carts overturned and people ran. The mountain's dark cloud leaned over the city.

"The world ends," a man shouted as the earth shook.

Vesuvius roared like a hundred cracks of thunder. More rocks fell, and the sun disappeared in a haze. I coughed against black ash, cloying and thick. I coughed again. Julia shoved a sleeve against her mouth. Using the sword, I knelt, cut away two long strips of her toga, and rose to wrap the cloth around our heads, covering our mouths. My cloth tasted of gritty blood.

Down the street, from where we had come, flames jetted sideways. A snarl sounded, and then a barking roar so loud it almost put Vesuvius' complaint to shame. Another shower of rocks fell. One beat into my thigh. Another slammed against my head, staggered me to the side. A blow across my back almost sent me to my knees.

"There!" I shouted to Julia, pointing. "Shelter!"

Taking her hand, I raced toward Apollo's broken temple, several hundred feet away. A form wavered out of the gloom, darker than night and as tall as a man. Mars' beast, grown to an impossible size, looked down at us with glowing eyes. It bore three heads on three necks sprouting from a single body. Two of

46

those heads dragged the ground between its front feet, charred ruins hanging low.

"The vessels must die," the remaining head rumbled, and the beast stepped forward on three legs. The fourth had been burned away.

Julia faced the beast squarely, grabbing at the icon about her neck. I still held her other hand. Sprinting away, I left her no choice but to follow.

"Wait," she called out, "I fear no beast of hell."

"I do," I answered, pulling her toward the temple as more skyrock fell and Mars loomed out of the darkness. "But I'm more afraid of its master."

Though in disrepair, due to an earthquake years earlier, the stone temple remained solid. It would provide shelter from the breaking sky and maybe protection from the mountain's dark cloud. Either way, the doorway would hinder the beast and god. They could only approach us from one direction.

We were not alone in seeking the temple. Half a dozen others raced for the same doorway, but when the beast roared they ran for other buildings.

Lungs burning, I shoved Julia through the opening, and turned, switching the sword to my good hand after releasing the whore. The beast limped forward. Mars walked slightly behind, looking not as svelte as he had before. Part of his clothing was burned away. The burnt fingers of one hand curled in ruin, but his mocking smile remained.

From behind, a thin spear poked past my side, its point wavering as it faced the pair. "Weapons hang on the wall," Julia said in my ear.

"Get back," I ordered.

"I won't let you face them alone."

"Fool woman. It's your death. I'll concentrate on the god. You go for the beast. It appears to only have

47

teeth and claws. I'm betting that, like the gods, it has become mortal."

As if in answer, Mars laughed. Blue fire jetted from the beast's nose. It's fire was not so powerful as the salamander's, but it terrified me. Against flames there is no defense.

"How humorous," Mars chuckled as larger stones fell and falling ash covered the street. Already, black soot lay over a foot deep. "Two mites daring to face down a god. I'd let you live for your courage, but my brother needs one of your souls for his cursed blade. Only a two-souled weapon can kill me, so you both have to die." He nodded to the beast. "Kill them."

After limping forward several paces, dragging the dead heads and dangling necks with it, the beast stopped. Cocking its remaining head to one side, it gave me a wink, and then twin jets of flame shot from its nostrils.

With no time to duck or dodge, all I could do was raise the Vulcan-made sword before my face.

The fire struck and parted.

I felt nothing as flames split around me, no heat, no force. Vibrating, my sword glowed with heat, first a dull yellow, quickly turning red. Too soon, it's thin edges melted and ran. I began to sweat, and then fire broke past Vul's god-built protections, driving me back a step and then two more as the leather clad hilt smoked.

I glimpsed a flash of motion at my side—the dart of a thrown spear—and the fire died away. Before me the beast wore a puzzled look as it fell to its knees. A small spear jutted from its chest. Growling, it staggered to three feet, lunged forward, and I shoved the glowing sword into its body.

The beast whimpered. Its skin sizzled. Its fur burst into flame as the sword went deep. Pulling the ruined blade free, I thrust again, and once more.

Standing in ash, Mars opened his mouth and roared. Around him, the falling ash split. Rocks bounded off an invisible shield. Raising an impossibly large sword, Mars ran toward me just as Vulcan stepped into view, the half-finished sword still gripped in his hand. His arm rose, the sword pointed, and a new flame broke from its tip, ripping forward, engulfing Mars. Vulcan cackled while Mars screamed, twisted about, and fled.

Wavering, I started to fall. Julia grabbed my arm and jerked me from the doorway.

"Fool," she whispered fiercely, beating her hands about my body. "You are burning."

"Run wife-stealer! Run!" Vulcan crowed from outside. "I'll show you power! I'll show you strength!"

"Family feuds are the worst," I muttered while Julia helped me stand. My back felt wet. I knew the whip wounds bled. My left hand appeared ruined, but some of the fingers still moved. Weak and tired, my vision swirled.

"Run and hide?" Julia suggested.

"You hide. I stand. After I'm dead, they might forget you."

"No. No." She shook her head. "Don't throw your life away for me. I'm a whore. A nobody."

"Run and hide," I ordered.

"Why sacrifice yourself?"

"I'm tired of killing. I'm tired of being afraid."

"I won't leave. My god will protect us."

The salamander slid through the doorway, followed by Vulcan. The deformed god held the wide-bladed, hilt-less sword, its steel glowing anew from Erius' fire. After blowing flame on a section of

49

the stone wall, Erius curled up against it and closed its eyes.

"Come, Atlus," Vulcan said. "Be reasonable. If I don't kill you, then my brother will. If not him, then you'll die when the volcano's foul air reaches Pompeii. You've been an obedient slave in the past. Give me your soul or take the woman's. My brother is charred, but I need a double-souled sword to make him die."

"If I were a reasonable man, I'd have killed the blasphemers," I told him, raising my blade. "Find another way to murder your brother because you can't have us."

"You would defy a god with a sword of his own making?"

I spat. "Good sword, weak-ass god, and you were a lousy master."

"That weapon won't kill me," Vulcan warned. His ugly lips twisted in a sneer. "It isn't double-souled." Grasping his weapon in both hands, he raised it over his head.

"Do three-headed dogs have souls?" I asked.

He paused. "What?"

I lunged. Twisting to the side, I caught his blade on mine, slid underneath, and shoved my half-melted steel through his heart. He stiffened, gasped, and my hands vibrated as something within the sword rushed into his body. Green lights, intertwined with muddy blue, swirled around him, dimmed, and were gone.

Seconds later, Vulcan slid free, fell to the floor, and died.

"Guess that three-headed dog had at least one," I said to Julia, looking down at the sword's remnants. Its once bright steel was carbon black and twisted. Opening my hand, I let it fall. "I've killed warriors and thieves and more than a few wild beasts. Even

50

killed an elephant once. Killing a god was easier than anything else."

Julia rested a hand on my shoulder. I flinched because my bleeding back hurt like a bitch, but she didn't notice.

"He was a pretender," she said. "Not a god."

"He traveled with a salamander and made swords that sucked souls. Close enough for me."

I felt weary, bone deep, soul sick weary. I had expected to die today. First came the argument between gods, escape, falling rock and ash, salamander fire, and everything else. I was tired of being afraid. I was bleeding and broken and had killed a god. I hadn't yet died, but knew I soon would. Outside, rocks still fell. Thick ash filled the air, stealing my breath. According to Vulcan, even fouler air headed our way.

Dry laughter broke through the gloom.

"Oh, gods." Turning my gaze, I faced the salamander.

Only it was no longer a salamander. Instead it owned a lizard's body and a man's malformed head. Looking at me, the creature released a vicious laugh.

"Well done, Atlus," he said. "I am pleased. Vulcan dead and Mars weakened. The last threats to my ascension almost gone. If I were a fair and just god, I would let you live, but I am not. You have killed one of us. For that you must die."

Bruised and bleeding, my sword a ruin, my body failing, I had no defense. "Hades?"

"No longer," the thing said, and his eyes glowed red. "For now and always, I will be known as God."

"Julia," I whispered. "Please run."

She did not run. Instead, she stepped to my side as Hades hissed, rose to its hind legs, and shot forth a column of fire shaming everything that had come

51

before. I tried to step before the aging whore, but she would not have it. Reaching to her neck, Julia jerked her hand forward. The cord holding her icon stretched, snapped, and she thrust her faith's worthless symbol against the flames.

I felt no magic, no secret forces. I felt nothing, and yet the fire parted, slipped to either side, curled back upon itself, and struck Hades in both his eyes. Screeching, the creature writhed in agony, but its fire continued, caught on a continuous loop while Julia faced the god of hell with nothing more than her blasphemous faith. Hades writhed, steamed, and screamed, until hell's fires dimmed, slowed, and were gone, taking the creature with them.

"My god will protect," Julia said as faint yells sounded. Rocks still crashed into the temple. Outside the door people clutched their throats and fell beneath the ash as Vesuvius' foul air stole their lives.

We were safe, Julia and I. Throughout that day, and the next, and the one after, she stood straight, holding her icon before her, creating a circle of safety.

Eventually the rocks stopped falling, the ash ceased, and Julia lowered her hand.

"The way is clear," she said with a voice both stronger and richer than anything I had heard before.

Then she fell.

I caught her, lifted her in my arms, and carried her into the streets of Pompeii and toward the gate that would take us far from this cursed city. A path led toward it, clear of ash and rocks, though a smooth-sided, black ash wall stood six feet high on either side of us. My damaged back and hand ached, but both felt whole.

"Mars was burned," Julia whispered, "but he still lives. He will want revenge."

I caressed the wooden tip of the icon she still clutched in her hand, a simple wooden cross attached to a worn leather thong.

"Mars is no danger," I told her. "Our God protects us."

Mark Eller spent twenty years happily writing stories and throwing them away. Then he met his future wife. She got mad about him throwing things away so he happily began writing books, publishing his shorts, and creating audio fiction podcasts, including *The Hell Hole Tavern, Mercy Bend*, and *The Turner Chronicles*. He can be found most days sitting in his man cave with his fingers busy typing new stories constantly running through his head. To find out more about Mark, go to markseller.com

SHUT UP AND DRIVE
by Timothy Reynolds
Chilean Earthquake, 2010

Juan sprinted through the downpour from the hangar to the Cessna parked out on the tarmac, soaked to the skin before getting halfway to the single-engine mine-hopper. He started his flight-worthiness circle check with the starboard wing, but his ex-wife's shout from the hangar stopped him.

"Eh! Just get the damned umbrella and come get us!"

He looked to the woman with the perpetual scowl flanked by their six-year-old daughters. At that same moment lightning struck so close, Juan's hair stood on end. In the brief second of stark, otherworldly illumination it seemed Consuelo and the girls were harsh, angry skeletons, judging him as inadequate. He shook his head to cast off the image and resumed his careful check of the aircraft's exterior.

"*Stupido!* Now! Or you can forget the girls coming to visit you at Christmas!"

No children at Christmas? First her infidelity broke his heart and now she would kill his spirit by taking his girls away? Was this what evil was? Juan surrendered and climbed up into the cockpit to fetch the umbrella. He was sure the aircraft was sound. He'd been up in it only last week and the flight to Bogotá was only two hours. He could get them to Consuelo's sister's third wedding and be back in time for lunch with his mother.

Thirty-two minutes into the bumpy flight, he gave up on trying to get above the storm and dropped down below the high ceiling of clouds to more rain but better visibility. The engine sputtered once, then continued whining just loud enough to drown out Consuelo's continuous complaining. Juan adjusted the fuel-ratio and listened for further hints of trouble as they ploughed through the deluge above the jungle. Little Isabel mimicked her mother by muttering something about hating the rain and then fell asleep like her sister.

Half-an-hour out from Bogotá the engine sputtered twice before quitting altogether. Juan frantically checked the gauges. No warning signs, no indicators of the problem. Frustrated, he tapped each of the dials and warning lights, hoping to shake up a loose connection in time to find a fix. When he tapped the oil pressure gauge, he got his answer. The needle immediately dropped to zero, and the warning lamp and buzzer went into full alert. He looked over at Consuelo and the girls, but they slept. Juan quickly kissed the crucifix hanging on the rosary around his neck and looked for a flat surface for an emergency landing.

The altimeter dropped quickly as the plane lost power. Juan was confident he could glide them down safely if he could only find a road or a field, until a bolt of lightning punched a hole through the port wing and the semi-controlled glide became a slow, inevitable spiral down into the Colombian jungle. The ground rushed up at them, and he unclipped his harness to reach around and hold his babies one last time.

The aftershock rattled the bus windows and tested the springs of the nearly retired Blue Bird school bus but Juan's brain was still reliving the crash five years ago. He closed his eyes again, took a deep breath and slapped himself hard across the face. The crash of the Cessna in Colombia was once again banished back to the world of his nightmares, but the slap setup a feedback loop through Juan's hearing aid. He tapped the aid. When that didn't work, he worked the on-off switch to reset it.

This was his sixth hearing aid since the crash that killed him, Consuelo, and the girls. Unfortunately he hadn't stayed dead, thanks to the old cocoa farmer who pulled him from the wreck a moment before the fuel ignited and the Cessna blew apart. With a combination of CPR and prayer, Juan was dragged back from the land of the dead badly burned, completely deaf in one ear, half-deaf in the other, and with a strange, wobbly limp. The day he left the hospital he changed his name to Miguel and left both flying and Colombia behind for Chile and a bus.

"Yo, Miguel! We just about ready to get this show back on the road?"

The young American preacher, Father Charles, stood in the doorway of the bus, having decided their roadside piss break was over and done. Juan looked at his watch. He'd only been asleep for two minutes, though it had felt like another lifetime within his nightmare.

"That was the second aftershock since we stopped so let's get moving and get to those quake-made orphans in Coronel where we can do God's good work."

He laughed at the last bit, and a dire chill run down Juan's spine despite of the midday heat on the Chilean back roads.

"*Si*, Padre. We can go as soon as everyone is loaded back up."

He looked around and noticed few of the twenty

57

international aid workers had actually gone more than a few steps from the bus. The aftershocks tended to send people running for cover or at least holding onto something a little more solid, but every one of this group stood around, unconcerned, taking slow drags on American cigarettes without much concern for the ground shimmying and shaking beneath them.

While his passengers butted out and loaded up, he walked around his bus, making a quick circle check, looking for loose bolts, leaks, or any one of the dozens of things that could spell disaster in an instant.

One of the pretty, young, German nurses approached and in near-perfect Spanish purred, *"How much further, Miguel?"* She put one slender, tanned, manicured hand on his scarred forearm, and his head nearly exploded with screams.

Papa! Don't go! Stay! Don't go with them!

Evil, Papa! Evil!

His knees weakened, and his belly clenched up. The voices he heard were little Isabel's and Giselle's. He looked around for his babies but saw only the tall, blonde, nurse looking nonplussed as if she hadn't heard the screams at all. The screams of the dead, the screams of the dying—the screams of his daughters!

He yanked his arm back, and the nurse's handprint on his old scars quickly faded from a new, ripe, red burn to white scar tissue. The new mark disappeared altogether, leaving only his old, puckered, scarred skin. The screams stopped when the contact was broken. Even though the tactile terror faded fast, his arm still burned. After a moment all was normal again, though the nurse watched Juan closely, her head tilted a little to the right.

"*¿Que pasa*, Miguel? Are you okay?"

Juan forced a smile. "I am fine, *señorita*.

"Okay, but you still did not answer my question.

How long?"

"Uh, we just passed Talca, *señorita,* so maybe five or six hours, if we're lucky. Probably closer to eight. Reports coming from the coast are saying the further west we go, the worse shape the highway is in. This quake was bad."

"Sixth largest ever recorded by a seismograph, handsome. It looks like 2010 is off to a fast start." She boarded the bus, sidling down the aisle to her seat.

Juan yanked his dirty red bandana out of his pocket and wiped his arm where she'd touched him. The effort didn't rid him of the dirty feeling nesting in his soul. He got back in his seat, wondering what the hell was going on.

The American preacher rounded up the last of the group and followed them up onto the bus. "Could have been there a lot faster if we'd flown, Miguel."

Juan nodded and started the bus. "*Sí,* that is true, but I do not fly and neither does my bus, Esperanza."

If he'd been completely honest with his customers he would have said he doesn't fly any more. If he were completely honest, he wouldn't be pretending to be a Chilean named Miguel, even though he was now probably more Miguel the half-deaf, crippled Chilean bachelor than Juan, the divorced, child-killing Colombian pilot.

"Well, just so long as we get there before midnight. I'd like to get to work with those poor souls while the moon is full and ripe."

Sporadic laughter came from around the bus, but Juan gave all of his attention to getting off the soft gravel shoulder and back on the roadway.

A little more than an hour later, Juan heard a voice just behind him and looked over his shoulder at the speaker, one of the three elderly nuns. She spoke so softly he couldn't hear her.

"*Un momento.*" He reached behind his ear and turned the hearing aid volume up as high as it would go. "*Sí*, Sister?" He kept his eyes on the road but leaned toward her to hear her better.

Her low voice sounded strong and clear. "I asked if you would care for a bottle of water, my son. I noticed you finished yours a few miles back." She held up a plastic bottle from one of the many cases the group had brought with them. "It's not cold, but it is refreshing."

"*Muchas gracias*, Sister." Juan reached up and opened his hand, not wanting to take his attention away from the trio of crashed and burned-out transport trucks they were passing. The bottle was placed firmly in his hand.

"Thank you." He quickly placed the bottle in the wire cup holder bolted to the dashboard and got both hands back on the steering wheel to get them around the mess of buckled and rough road.

"My pleasure, my son."

Holding on to the seat backs, the nun made her way back to her seat. Other than her shuffling footsteps, the bus was eerily silent as they rolled along. Juan looked up at the cabin-view mirror wondering if his passengers were rubbernecking at the accident but someone had tilted the mirror up so it pointed at the roof and not at the seats. Not wanting to spare a hand to unbuckle his seat belt and reach up to fix it while he drove, he left it in the odd position for the time being.

As they left the third wrecked truck behind them, Juan heard a low, beastly growl followed by a chuckle coming from the seats. *What in God's name?!*

That growl was answered with another. With a quick, worried glance over his shoulder, Juan saw his twenty passengers looking out the various dusty windows. The growl snuck up on him again. He concentrated on the sound and could distinguish words within the guttural utterance.

"All dead. Gone. Out of our reach."

Juan was confused. Who was out of reach?

"Yes, but be patient. The quake orphans are waiting. Amduscias has been busy gathering them from the surrounding ruined countryside."

Amduscias? Where had Juan heard that name before?

"King Amduscias? You trust him not to start without us?"

"I didn't say he hadn't. I told him one-in-twenty was his, just so long as his total for us topped one hundred and twenty."

"Will he find that many?"

"He was at two-hundred-eleven when we last spoke. He's been up and down the coast gathering together the lost, the broken, and the disenfranchised. He wanted to use his legions, but I reminded him we're not to draw attention to ourselves."

"If he's done this much on his own then he's welcome to his five-per cent."

"I'm sure his majesty will be so pleased he has your approval, Belial."

A deep chuckle followed before the two voices went silent.

Juan kept driving, trying to make sense of the strange conversation. Amduscias and Belial? He knew those names, but couldn't remember from where. The voices were those of his passengers, but at the same time, they weren't. He thought it was like having one of those United Nations translators repeating the Yugoslavian or French representative's words into Spanish a moment after they were spoken in their native tongue. Or was it all in his head? Were the heat and the thin mountain air messing with his mind? He shook it off and drove on.

A few miles down the road another bus lay twisted and shattered in the ditch where it had been tossed by the earthquake. A row of broken bodies lay next to the road. At least three people worked to retrieve more corpses from the wreck. Nearby, a turkey vulture rocked from foot to foot, waiting for a rescuer to turn his back so it could hop in and feed. Two of the rescuers lifted the body of a young girl out through a shattered window. All Juan could think of was his own dead babies and his role in their deaths. For five years he'd been berating and cursing himself for not finishing his pre-flight inspection, his circle check. He also cursed himself daily for allowing Consuelo to bully him into taking the easy way. He was sure he would have found the oil leak and either fixed it or postponed the flight and to hell with the stupid third wedding of a mean cow whose husbands would rather die of heart attacks and strokes than live another day with her.

"Earthquakes are the best."

He blinked away his self-pity at the sound of the growled revelation made behind him. The best?

"I used to like floods, but the pickings are too thin for the effort it takes."

"What about hurricanes?"

"Only if we can get there before the cleanup progresses too far. New Orleans was a mess. It was great. Enough suffering for all of us."

Enough suffering?

"January 23, 1556. Shaanxi Province, China."

"700,000."

"830,000 was our final total."

"Now *that* was a feast."

"I didn't feed like that again until the Calcutta cyclone in 1737."

"You were there? Me, too!"

Juan reached up and turned off his hearing aid. Who or what in God's name was he hearing? After a moment he turned his hearing aid on again, though he was terrified of what he was going to hear next.

"Why does that not surprise me, Dajjal?"

"Says she who never misses a meal. I'm surprised you weren't here during the actual quake, Lamashtu."

Lamashtu? Another name he'd heard once before? When he was young?

"There was an odd spike in the birth rate in Northern Africa, and I was needed to thin things out."

"Infants? Lucky you."

Stunned, disoriented, and nauseated by what he heard, Juan slowed the bus and pulled over on the shoulder. He needed air and silence. Dammit, he needed the voices to stop, wherever they were coming from.

"Hey, Miguel. ¿Que pasa?"

"Sorry. My, um, turn to piss. Maybe a good time for a smoke, too." He pushed on the metal handle and swung the door open, swapping the stifling heat of the bus for a little of the slightly cooler mountain air. As he stood, he nudged the cabin-view mirror down with his elbow until he was sure it would give him a good view of his passengers when he reclaimed his seat. Maybe if his eyes could see the lips moving with the words he heard, it would all make sense.

"Did I hear smoke break?" The German nurse was right on Juan's heels when he stumbled down the steps.

He limped around the front of the bus. Out of sight, he removed his hearing aid, bent over, and poured water over his head. He rubbed the warm wetness into his face and washed away the sweat salt and road grime, and then put his hearing aid back in.

"You okay, Miguel?"

He should have known he wouldn't be alone with this group. "The thin mountain air and no lunch, Padre."

"Well, my friend, that won't do at all. I'm sure between the twenty of us we can round up a little sustenance for our good driver."

"I'm fine, Padre, really. Much better now that I've had a little fresh air." He was damn sure he didn't want to share what passed for food with this group.

"Nonsense! I insist. As a matter of fact, I'm sure I have an apple you're welcome to."

"Padre..." He knew he was losing the argument.

"You need to eat, and a nice juicy Granny Smith will hit the spot. Don't tell me you're not at least a little bit tempted, Miguel."

Father Charles stepped back into the bus, and Juan's hearing aid picked up the preacher's low, growly whisper clearly through the open window.

"We have to keep the driver strong and lucid. We may need him to get us past any road blocks the military set up to keep the curious away from the worst areas. I need a Granny Smith apple and something substantial, like a sandwich."

Even Juan's faulty hearing aid couldn't clarify the following exchange of low growls, but a moment later Father Charles stuck his head out of the door. "Load up, people! We're over halfway there."

When Juan dropped down into the driver's seat the preacher handed him the promised apple, a plastic-wrapped sandwich, and a warm juice box drink.

"Hopefully this will help, my friend."

"Gracias. I am feeling much better now and will get us back on the road before I eat." Juan forced himself to accept the offered food and placed it down to the left of his seat.

"I don't want you distracted while you drive, Miguel. We can take a few more minutes here."

"Nonsense, Padre. If I cannot eat and drive at the same time, I would not be able to call myself a bus driver."

"Well, if you insist."

"I do, Padre. And thank the people who shared. I am blessed by their generosity."

"Think nothing of it."

Juan cranked the door closed, released the parking break, shifted Esperanza into gear, and was a little less gentle as he got his beloved bus back onto the black-top. The preacher returned to his seat.

Juan felt something bump his left foot and looked down quickly to see the apple rolling around. No way was he going to eat anything from the hands of these people. He crushed the apple under his heel to keep it from rolling around. He glanced up at the newly adjusted mirror to see if anyone had noticed his disdainful treatment of their gift. A horn honk on his left side yanked his attention back to the road before he could focus on their faces in the vibrating mirror.

Once the old Ford passed them and sped on, Juan shot a glance at the mirror and nearly screamed at what he saw. It could not possibly be what he thought. He blinked, rubbed his eyes quickly, and reached for the bottle of water. He might indeed be suffering from heat stroke for in that brief look into the mirror he was sure his passengers had all donned bizarre, horrific, Halloween masks.

He quickly looked back over his shoulder to confirm or deny the sight, but the faces looking out the windows or down into books and magazines were human faces. They were tired and hot and probably a bit hungry themselves, but they were human.

Remembering the conversations he'd been overhearing, he forced his eyes to look back up at the mirror. *¡Madre de Dios!* Clamping his jaw shut so he didn't utter the words out loud, he drove on, his hands shaking. As the miles rolled past, he stole occasional glances up at the mirror and his mind cleared, his resolve strengthened, and his hands eventually steadied. They were beasts!

Demons, Papa!

Isabel? Yes! And she was right. He looked at demons! Near the back was a handsome man—with bat wings! Where the German nurse had been, sat a hideous, human-sized viper. In the front seat an angel with the head of a lion read Jennifer Rahn's *Wicked Initiations*, the book he'd seen the Padre with. A bump in the road got Juan's attention for a moment, but his eyes flickered straight back to the mirror. He was certain of it. *¡Sangre de Cristo*, they were demons! It could be the only explanation! These were not masks he was looking at. Not a hallucination. It was...what? A vision? A sending? A glimpse into another reality? Was he dead? Was this Hell? Why him?

"You really should keep your eyes on the road, my friend. I moved that mirror up so you wouldn't get distracted by silly ideas."

"I...you..." He looked directly at the speaker. Father Charles crouched next to him, a very human Father Charles. He had neither lion's head nor angel's wings. He sweated and smiled, though the smile didn't reach his eyes.

"What? What are you thinking, Miguel? Or should I call you Juan? See, we all have our little secrets that aren't really secrets after all, my friend."

Juan shivered and stole a look at the mirror. A demon squatted beside him. "I'm not going to let you..." His brain tripped over itself as it tried to adjust to the information it received.

"Let us what, Juan? You'll do nothing. There is nothing you can do, so just shut up and drive." The tires on the right side of Esperanza grabbed at gravel, and the preacher gently placed his overly warm hand on Juan's head, turning his attention back to the road. "Maybe you should forget your *loco* notions and just do what you've been paid to do—take us to the earthquake survivors. You accepted my silver so you really have no choice."

Demons, Papa!

Juan kept his eyes front as Father Charles straightened from his crouched position, tore the mirror off its mount, and smashed it with his fist.

"Problem solved, Juan. No more delusions, illusions, or hallucinations. Let's just get to those poor orphans and render them all the succor we possibly can."

A dark, evil hunger stained the words, and Juan truly knew terror for the first time in a very long time. Not for himself, but terror for the children those creatures would find at the end of this journey. Horror for their innocent souls and the souls of anyone who would keep those beasts from their meals, or harvests, or whatever the hell they planned to do. Gripping the wheel until his knuckles nearly cracked, he guided Esperanza down the mountain road as it steepened and the curves became more pronounced. He slowed reflexively, not wanting to break an axle in a hole or skid into the rock face. His brain spun, lost in the enormity of it all.

A growly whisper came from the middle of the demonic pack he chauffeured. "There's nothing quite like the taste of a five-year-old girl's soul when she looks into my eyes and thinks she sees love while I drain her essence. Mmm hmm."

The highway edged close to the drop-off. Without a second thought, Juan, who had already died once in his lifetime, shifted his good foot from the brake pedal to the accelerator and guided his Esperanza, his 'Hope', through a quake-made rift in the guardrail and off the precipice.

Amidst the anguished screams and wailing fury of the demons behind him, the former pilot smiled peacefully and spoke his last thought aloud to no one in particular. "I really have missed flying."

Timothy Reynolds is an internationally published Canadian writer and photographer. His own ancestors danced in and around history (including being banished from Salem and involved in the Russian Revolution), so it's no surprise a common element in his writing is a blending of historical facts with fictional tales. He has experienced an earthquake, a hurricane, a twister, avalanches, and forest fires first-hand, yet it's the evil in mankind that scares him most. Find out more about Tim at:

tgmreynolds.com

LONDON PECULIAR:
THE SECRET OF THE FOG
by Steve Merrifield
The Great Smog of London, 1952

My Dear Jim,

If you received this letter then I have died before I got to see what 1953 was going to hold for me and my loved ones. I committed this letter to my solicitor. After my experiences on a cold, foggy December night with the dreaded fear I would not survive the month, he was to release it to you upon the event of my death.

I desperately wanted to speak to my beloved Barbara and you, my best friend, about my encounter and the terror it's caused me, but I feared you would both consider me mad. I am also telling you this because during the three years of that Hellish war we covered each other's backs. In some way I hope, although it is too late to save myself, this letter will, in some way, protect you.

I was on duty on a night shift at the beginning of the week. The night was thick with fog like we have been having so frequently recently, certainly living up to its nickname of London Particular. The night was bitterly cold with visibility down to a couple of feet, and the air reeked of sulphur and coal dust from the pollution trapped in the city by the fog.

I walked the quiet streets keeping close to the walls so as not to lose my bearings in the pale grey fog-smothered streets and open spaces turned into voids of swirling mist. I went about my duties rattling door handles of closed premises to check for unlocked doors on shops and residences ripe for thieving and looked out for signs of broken entries.

Even with the fog, the shift was pretty standard. I walked from police box to police box, warming myself as I could in those cold concrete shells on their small bar fires. I scored a free sandwich and a mug of tea from the lads working the night shift of Marshall's, the bakers, and found the usual pint left out for me on the window ledge at the rear of the Green Horn, which as ever went down a treat during a long stretch of the legs. I would like to add this was my one and only alcoholic beverage, so my perceptions were not altered by alcohol. After having supped my pint, the events I want you to know about occurred.

I continued on my way down the alley when my helmet was knocked clean from my head. I don't mind telling you, it startled me, though it was an old familiar cause, a length of black cotton stretched across the alley at helmet height. A spot of deliberate hat toppling mischief. No doubt some toerag having fun at a bobby's expense. I was able to laugh it off in the good nature I expected it to have been intended, though my mirth quickly gave way to vexation when I couldn't find my hard top in the bloody fog. I felt the air just above the ground, with caution as I didn't know what I might put my hand in. Staggering to and fro, bent in half, I searched for my hat. I heard a shuffling sound but didn't think much of it. I suspected a rat, the usual company in such a place. I carried on my folded over search when I heard a scuff. I froze as I was. Unless the vermin had size ten boots on, it was no rat.

Before I could rise up and challenge whoever it was to make himself known something emerged from the fog. A pair of battered, holey leather service boots with ragged trousers covering the legs above them stood less than a foot from my face. I staggered backwards to a safer distance and stood tall, one hand gaining a firm grip on the moulded handle of my wooden truncheon, the other extended with my torch directed at the man in the fog. I yelled at him, "Stop right there!"

The figure did indeed stop as I could hear no movement. However, I leapt away so effectively, I gained such distance I had lost the man in the fog. My torch light blazed back at me in the reflective moisture in the atmosphere. The alley was narrow and could barely be walked with three men abreast. Even with the surrounding smog, I was sure to spot him if he attempted to slink past me. I inched forward until I could see the man as a darker grey solid amongst the shifting pale mist glowing in my torchlight. I called out again to him.

"Who goes there? Come forward. Slowly."

The man did not move. The pair of us stood in the fog staring at each other's rough shape in a stand-off. During this time I noticed a peculiar phenomenon. The atmosphere seemed thicker around the man at chest height. It wouldn't have struck me as curious considering the fog can often be thinner at ground level, had I not been able to make out the scabby details of the bare black brickwork of the alley either side of him, which meant the fog was thicker around the man. Stranger still, the area of dense fog seemed to shrink and swell in a motion repeated, again and again. There was a rhythm to it, as though the fog around the man's chest and head pulsed. At first I wondered if the man were breathing heavily and could disturb the fog in such a way. Yet the time it took for the fog to dissipate then replenish

71

was too long for a man's breathing to have had an effect upon the air.

I found my own breath catching in my chest. I didn't know the intentions of my silent companion. He could have been a harmless vagrant or a criminal out to do mischief upon a copper stumbling across him on the job.

In the quiet, I became aware of a low wheeze and a whispering shush accompanying the disturbance of the fog. The whistling drag sounded as the fog thinned, while the rush of air sounded as the fog thickened as though the fog were indeed being breathed in and out within an unnatural respiration. I drew my truncheon. I am not quick to strike a man as you know, but something about this loiterer unnerved me. I warned him I was going to come closer. He did not flinch or answer. I continued inching forward to a point where details emerged from the haze.

The man wore a great woollen overcoat as tatty and worn as his trousers and boots. I could see in the light how his ragged clothes were moist and mouldering, caked in mud. I still couldn't see a face. Frustrated, I whipped my torch through the air to disperse the fog and finally saw the man's features, a cracked leathery face bristling with wild grey bedraggled whiskers, a face you and I would both recognise, Jim, Old Boy Charlie, the vagrant. I had heard he'd been found dead, choked to death like so many hundreds who had died this year because of the smothering, poisonous smog.

I breathed a heavy sigh of relief though. Old Boy Charlie was of no harm, was he? He might stink up the air, pester us for the price of a cuppa, or get to our window-ledge beers before we could, but no bother really. Standing down, my feet hit something that rolled away from me, my helmet. I stepped away from the tramp and retrieved my headgear from the ground. Dusting it down, I laughed at my fear, told the old fella I was glad the rumours of him pushing up the daisies were exaggerated, and asked what his business was in the alley. Thinking he would tell me I was in his doss, I popped my hat back on my head, only he didn't answer me. He just stared at me with dead eyes.

Dead, unblinking eyes.

Jim, it was Old Boy Charlie all right, but there was something different about him. At first I thought he was six sheets to the wind on account of him looking so stupefied. The blasted fog billowed around his face again, and I had to fan it away to get another good look. I described him as leathery earlier, never a more accurate description, except looking again, I saw more.

His face had the look of being an aged leather mask, to the point where all moisture had been lost, and the skin was cracking and brittle. His eyes still didn't move, and getting a good look at them, they seemed unhealthy. Not the plump wet orbs they should have been, they were withered saggy sacks, glistening more like congealed pus. I thought then maybe his death had been an exaggeration by someone who had seen him in this condition. He definitely didn't appear to be long for this world.

When something twitched beneath his beard, I knew I wasn't being studied by the spoiled eyes in his head, but by black glistening eyes writhing beneath his beard. I had little time to study and confirm what I glimpsed as the old boy suddenly swatted me aside with strength I had been unprepared for. I ended up with my legs sprawled out before me and my back slumped against the wall with a fierce pain in my hand. I had thrown my hands down to cushion my fall and thrust a palm down onto some broken glass, a bleeder of a wound which quickly covered me in crimson.

Charlie stepped over me without any word or regard and trudged out of the alley in his shuffling gait. With the clarity of pain cutting through the encounter, I found myself quickly challenging myself and concluded I must have misunderstood something I had seen in the man's grimy beard.

I left Charlie to make his slow escape, the priority to see to my injury, and with his tortoise pace, I knew I could catch him up. You and I each have about thirty years on him after all. I pulled the glass out, balled a hanky up in my hand to stop the bleeding, and set about recovering my footing as well as my truncheon and torch scattered from my fall. By the time I left the alley, I could just make out the shuffling silhouette of his body in the broad thick air of the street, although his head and shoulders were obscured.

With Old Boy Charlie marking my way in the pea soup, I ran at him, ready to nick him and take him down the station, although a warm cell and a comfy bed wouldn't be much punishment for a man suffering the cold hard streets and exposure to the harsh elements. The cool moist air pressed against me as I rushed through the atmosphere, the oily chemicals trapped in the fog slicked my face, inside my mouth, and stung my eyes. In my haste, I lost all thought of safety and the dangers of the fog.

Something squealed at me with a deafening pitch before I was struck bodily with such a force I found myself thrown to the tarmac. The air was knocked from me and the half of my body that had taken the hit was a sickening mixture of numb and aching. Twin roundels of light topped by two sets of paired rectangles of light high above my prone body, along with the roar and tick of a diesel engine, told me I had run out before a Routemaster.

The driver yelled down at me from the cab in a mix of anger and fright, and the conductor scrabbled across the deck to come to my aide. I didn't listen to them, for my quarry was similarly sprawled out beside me several feet away. Strange fog swirled around him at ground level while it didn't seem to be around me or the road and paving about me. I suspected it hung around him for the same reason it had clung about his shoulders and head, whatever the reason might have been. I didn't have much strength in me after the shock and actual harm of my run in with a double-decker bus, but I had enough to crawl over to Charlie.

My intention was to check if he wasn't too badly off, cuff the bugger, and arrest him for assault. Although, despite his attacking me, I still hoped the old sod would be all right. With much complaint from my injured arm, leg, and back, I rolled onto my front, careful not to put any pressure on my cut hand, and made a hobbling crawl over to Charlie.

He was still.

I leaned over him and stared down into his fog wreathed face. I ignored the conductor who ran up behind me and cycled through a pattern of asking how Charlie and I were, swearing, and extolling the names of Jesus, Mary, and Joseph. Charlie opened unblinking eyes, and his death mask face did not react to me addressing him. I called louder as though Charlie were down a hole. He didn't respond. I glanced down at the beard and remembered what I *thought* I had seen. With my good hand, I dared to touch his greasy beard and parted the course grungy fibres. Something warm and wet moved against my index finger. I flinched away from it, jumping so hard

I nearly fell back on my rear, and the conductor yelped in succession.

A glossy black orb twitched beneath the beard. An eye. An inhuman eye. Disgusted and disbelieving in equal measure, I recovered my truncheon and slid its shaft under his beard and lifted it away. Eight black eyes wriggled on a pale fleshy proboscis. I leapt away, scrambling backwards to put some distance between me and *it*.

Jim, I know we saw some terrible things in service, horrendous injuries, bodies, and remains of bodies in conditions most people would only expect to see in animals within an abattoir, but we could prepare ourselves for such sights by imagining the effect of shredding bullets or explosives. In no way could I have prepared myself for what I saw in Charlie. I lost all comprehensible speech.

The conductor, somewhat recovered from the shock of the accident, decided to see what had startled me so. He leaned over Charlie and gasped. He must have seen the eyes. I didn't get to find out as a great geyser of thick fog erupted from beneath Charlie's chin and engulfed the man's head. He reared and staggered away clutching at his throat. A bloated tongue stuck out of the conductor's widely stretched O of a mouth, emitting a dreadful death-rattle from deep within him. I could see his face even in the poor fog-shrouded light of the Routemaster's headlights, and he was blue.

He collapsed to the ground and became still. The driver leapt out of the cab and flung his peaked cap through the air as he dashed to his chum's side. I warned him to stay away from the old man. All the driver could say over and over again was his mate was dead.

Charlie rolled over onto his front and wriggled in place a few moments; as though he had forgotten how to use his arms and legs. He lifted himself to his knees and took several precarious steps on uncertain legs before he continued in the direction he had been heading. I glanced up at the street sign beside me and saw his direction was taking him towards the fog shrouded heart of Trafalgar Square. I limped after him, and it seemed Old Boy Charlie's pace had picked up as the gap between us took longer for me to close.

When I did reach him, I knew it was pointless to call his name or to try and communicate with him. Charlie was indeed dead. I began to suspect he had been dead when the bus hit him. He had been dead when I initially stood in his way in the alley. He had, in fact, died as I had heard several days before. Charlie was the walking dead. Not like I had seen in a Bela Lugosi movie before the war. I hadn't seen or heard of anything like this except in the tropics where we fought, Jim. Remember those briefings on the wildlife which could be just as dangerous as a Jerry or a Jap bullet? Bites containing diseases, insects that saw us as walking meals, creatures that could use us as living hosts for their young?

I was about to make a move on Charlie to confirm what I fearfully suspected when I heard a shuffling from behind me. I turned and saw just fog. I heard a step to my side and again found only the shifting smog. I wrongfully comforted myself with the idea it might be the driver and perhaps a passenger or two. I continued after Charlie who had once again become an indistinct shape in the mist. I recognized I was in the great expanse of Trafalgar Square and was completely obscured from the road, isolated from help, and without a sense of place or direction in the vast void of whiteness surrounding me. I was quite lost.

The headlights of another large vehicle swept from the distant road and passed through the fog, it refracted into a greater light in the moisture of the atmosphere and plucked shapes from the nothingness. All about me I could see the silhouettes of shambling men and women, all seeming to be heading to converge on one spot. The sounds I had heard earlier suddenly informed me it would be the same scene behind me and to my other side. I was within a closing crowd of the walking dead.

With the passing of the headlights, I was lost in the dark murky fog. I had lost sight of Charlie too. I walked ahead in the direction he had been heading, with a firm grip on my truncheon, and I struck out at the first patch of darkness to emerge from the mist. I swung at head height. I reasoned I did not need to worry about killing a man already dead. The wooden shaft hit something fleshy, not the solidness of a skull, yet I could see in the fog wafted thin by my sudden movement, I had clubbed at Charlie's head.

The vagabond turned toward me. His weathered face split apart, the start of a process of collapse his whole head underwent from my blow, as though I had struck a hollowed out sun-dried melon. Clumps of his face and scalp folded away and hung about his shoulders revealing a fleshy pale pulp within. In the light of my torch, I watched in disgust as the row of black eyes tucked into his neck rose up on a ripple of the flabby muscle. More proboscises shivered out and up from beneath the collar of the old man's coat and shirt. Chubby tubes retracted slowly into flaccid folds of skin, taking with them a protracted whistling suck of the air as I had heard in the alley earlier. Some moments later, they swelled and coughed a single blast of fog out from them.

Suspecting this would occur and that being engulfed in this sudden wash of fog would end me as it had the conductor, I ducked down and scrambled away. Attuned to this sound of inhalation and exhalation, I realised I could hear it all about me. The people in the fog were inhabited by the same grub like creatures, and they were all intent on gathering at this spot for a purpose I could not understand until the swipe of headlights again aided me. I saw what lay ahead of me, and what grub-Charlie returned to pursuing.

A great thing as big as a single-decker bus sat upon the ground before me, its silhouette irregular and constantly shifting. I shone my torch and found a gigantic naked version of the grub that had spawned, grown, and consumed its way through Charlie, sprawled out before me on the paving slabs of Trafalgar Square. Its vast underbelly clustered with fleshy stumpy probes that could have acted as feet to propel it, but with it being static they seemed content with drumming the ground with soft pats of the concrete. Its fleshy sides segmented into deep folds brimmed with larger tubular proboscises pumping fog into the atmosphere at the same rate as its spawn. The atmosphere was a product of those creatures! A crown of proboscises mounted with black glistening eyes languorously wavered in the air high above me.

I could only stand dumbstruck in this great beast's presence and witness the grub-Charlie press itself against the giant's side. In less than a minute, Charlie's remains had been sucked away by the monsters proboscis, absorbed into the folds, revealing the grub within the tramp to be a miniature of the larger thing before me. I felt unthreatened by the

79

giant while the emergent creature proceeded to suckle at the beast's side. I watched for ten minutes, and in that time all the other walking dead converged on the beast, were stripped of their husks of humanity, an occurrence I fear takes place all around the city during a London Particular.

The event seemingly over, the great whale of a grub arched, and a flicker of light played along its body. The creature dissolved into the fog as it transported itself to another place. I thought I had survived, then I considered what I had witnessed; the equivalent of fish following an inbred instinct to return to a spawning ground, part of a reproductive process beginning with spores carried within the fog, breathed in by us, where the parasite would root and grow, instantly or gradually choking its unsuspecting victim to death. Taking several days to mature it would feast on its host and then reanimate its host's corpse to migrate in answer to the imperceptible call of its parent.

The next day, as I write this, I realise I have not survived. I have a cruel pain in my chest, and I have begun to dread something is inside me, already living off me. If you are reading my account of this fantastic event, then the grub within me has already matured, and I will soon rise again as grub-George. I tell you this so you can take precautions, and convince your loved ones and mine to do the same. Perhaps tell the Sarge. Hell, perhaps you should tell the army and Churchill too. Warn them Jim, warn them to beware the fog!

Steve Merrifield is an English writer who writes UK-based tales of horror. His influences are *Hammer Horror* movies, the gothic 70's episodes of *Doctor Who*, and the writers Shaun Hutson, Clive Barker, and H.P. Lovecraft. Steve currently has four e-books of urban horror to his name, *Ivory, Harvest, The Pack,* and *The Room.* With a series of short stories *The Darkwood Mysteries,* tales of Victorian horror & adventure on their way with many more e-book titles planned for the future. To find out more about Steve, go to:

<u>www.stevemerrifield.co.uk</u>

TILL DEATH DO US PART
by Laurel Anne Hill
Berkeley Fire, 1923

Gusts of hot northeast wind swept across Berkeley, threatening to scatter Luke's ashes over the amber hillsides. Nelda wouldn't let that happen. The chunky mess of spousal charcoal in her galvanized bucket was headed for a far more fitting final resting place—the septic tank of the furnished rental cottage she'd shared with Luke since 1913. Nelda's grip on her garden trowel tightened. Till death do us part and good riddance.

"I'll get ya for spoiling my luck," Luke had said. *"Roast ya alive, I will."*

Nelda never would forget the way Luke had bellowed at her, but he'd spoiled his own luck, croaking the night he'd hollered those words. September 10, 1923, six days ago. Rotten louse. Why had she put up with the likes of him for ten years? Remaining a spinster in Michigan would have been preferable.

Now, forty and wiser, she knelt in the dirt beside the open clean-out portal of her septic tank. Inhaling the stench of sewer gases, she remembered Luke's brown, whiskey-wild eyes, the iron crowbar he'd wielded, and the smash of glass when he'd missed her, demolishing a table lamp.

Threaten to roast her, would he? Two days ago Nelda signed the papers and had his corpse cremated instead of buried. Oh, sweet irony.

An icy chill seeped into the back of her neck as though someone pressed a wad of snow there. She could almost see Luke's dilated pupils stare at her from a nearby potted nasturtium. Her hand trembled. What was it her mother used to say about creepy premonitions? Oh, yes. A good thing the dead stayed dead.

Enough scary thoughts. Time to dispose of her late husband, may the devil keep his soul. Nelda dipped her garden trowel into the bucket. Metal scraped metal. She lowered a trowel of Luke's remains into the septic tank's malodorous hole, tilting the tool's tip downward.

"This is for the black eye you gave me five years ago," Nelda said, enunciating each word, "when you thought I was knocked up."

She scooped another batch of her deceased husband out of the bucket. Lord, that sewer stench was enough to make her retch. A strand of her red hair dangled in Nelda's eyes. Her bony knees ached. Even in death, Luke and misery went together like poison oak and itchy skin.

"And this is for all the money you wasted on speakeasies and bootleg liquor."

Then there was the tooled leather box, the size of a pocket tin for chewing tobacco, Luke's so-called lucky box, his usual excuse for slapping her down. They'd had a good marriage until he'd found that damn box in an alley downtown. Lord, right from the start he would have killed her if she even dusted it. She never dared to touch the thing until after Luke lay dead in a heap on the living room floor. Just moving the container from his jacket pocket to a bedroom drawer had triggered nausea and the shivers.

More trowels full of Luke led to more wretched memories of him and his weakness for hooch. His feet should have stumbled underneath his inebriated pot-bellied hulk and let her brick hearth crack open his worthless skull years ago. At least that had finally happened. Amen. She may not have murdered him, but she sure hadn't run next door to phone for medical help until he'd stopped breathing.

The remainder of his remains slid down the clean-out. Nelda straightened her back, set down her trowel, and shoved the concrete cover of the entry port into place. He wouldn't—couldn't—hurt her now. She could live the rest of her life in peace, the only good to have ever come from Luke's shameful worship of John Barleycorn.

How fitting, him burnt like a peanut-butter cookie left too long in a hot oven. How delightful, his ashes coating a cesspool full of crap. A shame Luke's pill of a soul, already frying in Hell, would never know.

Nelda pushed soil back over the clean-out area, the taste of sewer vapor stuck to her tongue like glue. Her treatment of those ashes would have shocked her landlord, him being Catholic and all. Plus his wife, Betty, once had told Nelda the local parish priest forbade cremation. No sense in Nelda making more trouble for herself. A half-dozen pots of nasturtiums would camouflage the disturbed ground. She walked toward the garden shed to retrieve a few more potted posies. A blast of scorched wind hit her face, as though Satan arrived with a calling card.

Nelda could almost hear Luke's throaty voice whispering in her ear. *"Wind from the Devil's ass."*

Another chill coated the back of her neck, maybe from her own evaporating sweat. Nelda brushed dirt off of her shabby, black boots, one shoelace practically worn down to threads. September 16, 1923. Nelda must remember today until the moment she died, particularly if she ever got the foolish notion to fall in love again and get hitched.

"Oh, ya'll remember today, all right." Luke's voice

rose inside her head, realistic as blazes. *"Tomorrow, too."*

An icy shiver shot across the backs of her shoulders. Luke could have been talking straight at her.

The man in a three-piece suit crept up on Nelda's cottage mid-afternoon while she peeled turnips. She watched him from the kitchen window. Tall and thin, he was, like death's shadow, a derby hat wedged atop his head. Mr. Avery Green, her landlord, had come snooping.

He probably wanted to know if she planned to stick around now that Luke was gone. Well, that would depend if Nelda could take in more sewing jobs and figure out where her husband had stashed his drinking money. She'd found no loose planks in the floor when she'd hunted for them, and no wallet attached to the underside of furniture. She smoothed the skirt of her blue cotton dress, and then opened her front door and greeted Mr. Green.

"My deepest condolences regarding your husband." Mr. Avery Green lifted his felt hat off his balding head but only for a moment. "It pains me to discuss business matters at such a solemn time, but..." He cleared his throat.

Talking about money pained Mr. Green—a banker—about as much as devouring an ice-cream cone pained a ten-year-old boy on a hot summer's day. The old miser probably referred to the rent, due ten days ago. Luke must not have paid again. Not good news.

"Won't you come in and sit down?" Nelda's hand fidgeted with the pocket of her flowered percale apron. Better he parked his bony bottom in her living room than pondered why potted nasturtiums sat over the septic tank zone.

She excused herself and stepped into her bedroom. Her hands rummaged through her sack of washed menstrual rags in the tiny closet. Ah, here it was, the rag containing her emergency money. She retrieved four five-dollar bills and took them to Avery Green, who still wore his hat.

"Didn't your husband tell you?" Mr. Green's face flushed a ruddy color. "I raised the rent two dollars plus you owe me for August. He last paid me on July tenth."

Two dollars, plus a whole month? She owed twenty-four clams more? First the cost of the cremation and now this. Every cent in her meager checking account was already spoken for. All her emergency cash would be gone soon. Only Luke's drinking money would remain, if there was any left and she could find it. Damn Luke for not mentioning the unpaid rent or the increase, as though money matters were none of a woman's business. Now what was she going to do?

"Oh." How weak her voice sounded. "Luke didn't tell me."

"Shall I come back?" Mr. Avery Green said. His thick mustache almost twitched. "When your mind and affairs are better settled?"

Did she want him coming back anytime soon, looking around, inspecting every nook and cranny? What if he lifted the pots of nasturtiums, saw the disturbed soil, asked if there had been trouble with the septic tank? Could the lumpy parts of incinerated human remains be differentiated from sewage if he had the tank pumped out? And Nelda had placed Luke's funerary urn in the garden shed. Mr. Green might evict her if he discovered the container. She'd never find another affordable place in such a pleasant neighborhood.

Yet Luke could owe additional debts Nelda didn't know about. If she paid Mr. Green the twenty-four dollars, she would have nothing left to provide token payments to other creditors.

"If you could please wait another week," she said, "that would help."

Mr. Avery Green peered down his nose at her, as though she were a bug to be squashed. He tipped his hat, then left, and disappeared from sight up the hill. Why had he raised her rent? Her entire cottage, once used to house his gardener, could have fit into his parlor. He didn't need more money.

Tight as granny knots, her innards were. Nelda walked around the perimeter of the cottage. One of the pots of orange nasturtiums sat several inches from the spot where she had placed it, but her landlord hadn't headed in this direction at all. Who had moved the potted plant? And why?

She returned the flowers to where they belonged. The next breath of air felt hot in Nelda's lungs, as though she'd walked into a burning building. An instant later the back of her neck turned cool as an icebox.

"Ya know damn well who moved the plant," Luke's voice said.

Couldn't her ears stop pretending to hear her deceased husband speak? The dead stayed dead, well, except for a few people in Bible stories. Furthermore, Betty had claimed cremation interfered with any sort of resurrection. Death had taken Luke and couldn't give him back. These strange goings-on must have a reasonable explanation.

The clock on the living-room mantel chimed seven. Daylight faded. Nelda glanced toward the bedroom where Luke's empty urn currently resided. She'd moved the vessel, a little larger than a wastepaper basket, out of the garden shed and into her closet. From where she sat, despite all her scrubbing, dark stains of his dried blood were still visible on her brick hearth.

Luke's leather box sat closed in her lap, the cowhide container the shape of a hip flask, only with a lid—about the dimensions of a man's thumb—instead of a screw-cap on the end. She shook the box secured by a small latch. No rattle meant no coins. What about folding money?

Somehow, this lucky-turned-unlucky box had destroyed their marriage. She should toss the blasted thing into the garbage can. No, this was the only place left in the house or garden she hadn't searched for dough. She needed to do this.

Nelda leaned back against her threadbare overstuffed sofa, her fingers stroking the box's tooled leather sides. An odd pattern, the narrow, slanted markings shaped like a sleepy cat's eyes. Were they why she felt something watched her?

"I'll toast your liver for lunch if you ever open this box," Luke had said.

Nelda's stomach twisted at the memory of Luke's threat. As soon as she could scrape together enough money for a train ticket, she would escape this memory-haunted place and stay with her sister in Nevada, maybe even return to Michigan. She was a respectable widow, after all, not a divorcee. Yes, someone in her family would offer her a room until her finances improved.

Her fingers unlatched the top of the box and raised the lid. Empty. The box was empty. Nelda exhaled with a groan. Her shoulders—no, her entire body—sagged. Luke had run out of luck, all right, and he had run out of money. No wonder he'd been so crazy furious the final night he'd attacked her. He'd craved more booze and knew he'd have to wait until his next payday at the machine shop to buy some.

Would that she had a payday. A train ticket to Nevada was apt to cost at least fifteen dollars, maybe even twenty or more. Doing mending never paid well, and she wasn't much good at typing or numbers. Where would she get the money she needed? By not paying Mr. Green? His wife, Betty, had always been nice to her, brought her homemade cookies and other treats. Nelda hated to cheat them out of their due, even if he was a snoopy banker. She set the box on the sofa. No use bothering to reattach the lid. Nothing was going to fall out of the container.

The smell of boiled vegetables reminded her she hadn't eaten dinner. A bowl of onions and mashed turnips might make her feel better. She picked up the leather box and lid to put them away. But what was this? Folded up, way down in the container's bottom? She turned the box upside-down and tapped the upper rim several times against the lamp table to loosen up the contents. Her first finger dug out a folded piece of paper money.

Ten clams. No, two bills were folded together. Twenty whole dollars. She hadn't noticed the dough earlier. She must have been too upset to see salvation right under her nose. Tomorrow afternoon she would head for the sixteenth street train station in Oakland and purchase a ticket to Nevada.

Luke must have been too plastered to have noticed the money. What a loser, had been since their third wedding anniversary, the night he'd found the leather box. Now Nelda was the lucky one. She would pack her clothes, pay her rent, and surprise her sister with a long-overdue visit. Oh yes, she'd take a good long piss on Luke, as well.

Twenty lucky dollars plus thirty from her emergency stash—fifty clams was so much money, practically her entire fortune. Nelda didn't want to carry it all in her purse. The carpet bag packed with her clothes also would be an easy target for a clever thief. She stood in a pool of afternoon sun in her bedroom and slid twenty-two rent dollars into her homemade shoulder purse. The rest of her cash should go back into the leather box. Paying Mr. Green and walking to the train station in Oakland would take hours. She'd better button the box inside the secret inner pocket of her charcoal-gray coat and wear the garment despite the day's heat.

Nelda yanked the lid off of Luke's lucky box. No, it was her lucky box now. A rolled-up ten-dollar bill practically flew out of the container and landed on the floor. Another ten spot remained inside. The money had not been in there last night. What the heck was going on? Two in the afternoon and she was twenty bucks richer? September 17, 1923 would be another day to remember.

The icy pressure against the back of her neck returned. The air in the bedroom heated up like an oven set to bake bread. She inhaled with a half-gasp. An odd scarlet light shone from her closet, through the opening where the door sat ajar. She'd never seen such a light in this house before—or anywhere else. Something was wrong. Terrible wrong. She peered inside the closet and faced Luke's urn. The pottery vessel glowed iridescent, crimson as blood.

"The dead stay dead," Luke's voice said. *"Except*

when they don't." The urn's glow intensified and pulsed.

Luke. Dear Lord, Luke was here, or at least part of him. Right here in this bedroom. He'd cheated the devil and come back—come back to get her. She had to get the blazes out of this cottage. Now!

Her lucky box, the money in her hand, they were hers, not Luke's. She stuffed them both into her secret pocket, grabbed her purse and bag, and raced through the living room and out the front door. She smelled smoke, heard crackling. To the northeast, dense coal-black smoke billowed over the ridge into the Berkeley Hills from the direction of Wildcat Canyon. Voices up the street shouted.

Up the road, Mr. Green's wife, Betty, stood in her fancy front yard, just stood there in a frilly dress and stylish heels like a statue in a park. A few feet away from her the crown of an oak burst into flames. A fiery spinning object—a shingle—plummeted from the sky and landed on her roof.

"Run, Mrs. Green," Nelda shouted. Clinging to her purse strap and carpet bag, Nelda hurried toward Mrs. Betty Green.

"Ya won't escape," Luke's gruff voice whispered.

Another blazing shingle landed on the Green's roof. How could this horrendous fire—this very real fire—have started? Luke was dead. He couldn't have set it. Nelda reached Betty, who held a small handbag atop her framed wedding photo as though the purse were a potato on a dinner plate.

"This way," Nelda said, motioning with her carpet bag. She slipped the long strap of her purse over her head, then tugged Betty's arm. "Follow me."

"My home!" Betty Green cried. "My home!"

A shower of sparks rained to the ground two feet away from Betty. The woman screamed, trying to stamp them out with her high-heeled shoes.

Nelda pulled her. "We've got to go," Nelda urged. "Please let me take you to your husband, to the bank where he works."

Betty's blue-gray eyes looked unfocused, dazed. Wind whipped her silver-streaked brown hair. The woman wasn't going to do anything, must be in shock. Nelda threaded her arm around Betty's and guided her away from the house, the crackling and popping roof ablaze.

"I'll fry ya to a crisp, I will." Luke's voice grew louder.

Nelda knew she mustn't panic. Control wasn't easy, though. At least Betty didn't appear to notice Luke's voice, but then, Nelda was who Luke had returned to haunt. Still, some sort of barrier had to separate life from death. Otherwise, ghosts would float everywhere and always bump into people. Luke's presence may have chilled the back of her neck, yet he probably hadn't touched her. She crossed the street at a brisk pace beside Betty Green, glancing around, the heels of their shoes clicking against the roadway.

The all-too-real inferno appeared headed for the University of California. She needed to move upwind, escape through the upper border of the conflagration instead of getting trapped in the middle. The best direction to aim might be uphill and into the wind but away from where the fire had started. When it was safe, she would leave this hilly section of northern Berkeley, arc around and approach the flat part of town from the south where Mr. Green's bank stood. Maybe later he would drive her to the train station in Oakland, although a big fire in the area would likely bog down traffic and delay train service.

She coughed from the smoke. Hot, she was so hot. Oh, to take off her coat. A bent, graying man wearing a plaid shirt and cotton trousers sprayed water from a garden hose onto his roof. Down the hill, where she had been just minutes before, a burning oak tree toppled. Sparks exploded like holiday fireworks. A power line had fallen and tangled in the tree's branches. Chimes rang. The Campanile bells on the University's campus. Sirens sounded in the distance. At least help was coming.

Lower on the hill and to the east, flames leaped onward, away from Nelda but in the direction of downtown Berkeley. Sprays of yellow cinders glittered like giant fireflies. This was like Hell on earth. The devil had come here and brought a piece of Hades with him. Luke must have snuck out in the process. She needed to think real clearly. He wanted to burn her and might try to ride the flames. If so, he could only travel in the direction of the wind. Dear God, don't let the wind shift.

"Avery," Betty Green said. She came to a dead stop, her hand over her mouth, as though she might vomit. "What if Avery tries to come up this way and find me? He'll be killed."

"Won't he have to stay at the bank?" Nelda said. "To keep order?" Before heading downtown, she and Betty should wait until the firemen quenched some of the flames.

"Oh," Betty wailed, "you don't know what he's like, always fretting about me."

Mr. Avery Green might be worried about his wife's safety, but Luke wanted Nelda dead. Nelda had to stay clear of the blaze. Still, Betty's face turned paler and paler, despite the heat. She looked as wilted as a plucked poppy baking in a pool of sunshine. At the corner of a main street leading toward downtown Berkeley, Nelda stopped. Should she walk in an arc according to her earlier plan or go directly toward the bank?

"Please," Betty begged. "I'll never forgive myself if something happens to Avery because of me."

"I'll get ya." Luke's voice again, so shrill Nelda's teeth ached. He wanted her caught in those flames.

"We'll go directly downtown on this street, then." Nelda pointed south, away from the hills. The cold feeling, the death feeling, pressed against the back of her neck.

"Avery'll walk up the next street over," Betty said, "I know he will. That's the route he always drives home. It's his favorite."

"The fire could reach there soon," Nelda said.

Betty already was on her way, purse in hand, unsteady in her ankle-strap high heels, wedding photo wedged under her arm.

The sky above Nelda exploded, like falling bombs detonated mid-air. Crazy-eyed people screamed, some carrying children away from the smoke and flames, others dragging pillowcases overflowing with possessions. The air above the Berkeley Hills grew hotter and hotter, as though the sun fell. Firemen pumped water, and still the fire raged. There was no walking down Mr. Green's favorite street anymore.

"We have to go toward the bay," Nelda shouted.

Such a roar around her, like being in the middle of a world war battle and a blast furnace rolled into one. Betty sobbed into her hand, head bent down, her wedding picture still tucked under one arm. She wobbled as she walked. Those fancy shoes weren't much good except at a party. A flaming shingle shot out of nowhere. Nelda pushed Betty out of the approaching missile's way.

The shingle exploded in the air above. Cinders rained. Nelda smelled singed hair. The ends of her red hair had caught fire. Her hand released her carpet bag and batted cinders from her locks and shoulders. She dropped to the ground and rolled. The next fiery shingle landed on Betty, setting her frilly sleeve ablaze. Screaming, Betty ran toward Nelda. A huge flame leaped between them, looming larger and larger. The flame had a face—a big, ugly, sneering face with shimmering yellow eyes. Luke's face. No body. Just his face and the devil's eyes.

"How much ya want to save her?" Luke said. *"Enough to return my box? Enough to die right here and now?"*

Nelda's eyes and imagination weren't playing tricks on her. Luke wasn't calling to her from some mystical doorway to the great beyond. His soul, in the form of flaming shingles and cinders, had touched her and Betty, had moved beyond the life-death barrier. He'd come back. All the way back.

How dare he come back! Damn Luke. Damn her marriage. Damn the leather box, even if she had found dough in it. Nelda didn't need miracle money anymore. She needed to survive this disaster and help Betty, to free herself from everything associated with Luke in the process.

Nelda fumbled with the buttons on her coat, pulled the coverless lucky box out of the secret pocket and hurled it at Luke's face in the flames. The box spewed out a cascade of water, as though it were a fire hose, dousing Luke and Betty. The fire on and around the landlord's wife sputtered, extinguished. Betty lay curled on the street, screaming, blisters welling up on her arms and cheeks. Another shingle sailed through the air in Nelda's direction. Luke's fiery face rode the shingle and bellowed out a vicious laugh.

Nelda coughed and bolted toward the bay. It didn't matter what Betty might think of her, getting left behind. Nelda had to put distance between herself and other people, let the flames of Luke's hate and rage fall directly upon her. She ran, her boots pounding the ground hard, her long-strapped purse bouncing against the front of her coat, her carpet bag left behind. Yet her fingers curled around something. The leather box! Hadn't she thrown the container into Luke's flaming face? How had the box returned to her?

Well, she would rid herself of the box once and for all. She tried to open her hand and drop the container. Her fingers clutched the thing even tighter than before. The lucky box refused to be cast aside. Even worse, it emitted a curl of black smoke and the stink of sulfur. The box was the devil's property.

Luke's hideous laugh blended with Betty's piercing screams. Nelda had to outrun those sounds, shut them out of her mind. A train, she would flee to the sixteenth street station in West Oakland and take a train. Ride to somewhere, anywhere but Nevada or Michigan, anywhere that didn't contain people she cared about, people she knew, people Luke could set afire to hurt her.

Betty still screeched. From some dark, painful place she pleaded for Nelda's help, as though hit by another blazing shingle. The very act of running away from Betty to keep her safe resulted in the dear woman's torture. The box—which Nelda had tried to get rid of but couldn't—was evil, would bring evil no matter what Nelda did. Because she had taken its money the way Luke had?

Till death do us part. Only her own death would bust her free of Luke or the box now. That's why Luke hadn't set her afire. He knew Heaven would

97

claim her soul and separate her from him, unless she did something bad, like take more of the devil's money or kill herself. Self-murder was still murder, or so her mother used to say. Yes, that was it. Luke intended to drive her crazy enough to commit suicide. What a bastard!

Nelda planned to survive. After all she'd endured, she deserved to live and find freedom, too. Just because the box wouldn't leave her didn't mean she had to use the money it gave her, didn't mean she would keep on bringing harm to people, or turn into another Luke. Did it?

"I got ya," Luke shrieked. *"I put the fix on that box when ya tossed it at me and it'll stick real good to ya now. Yer never gonna resist the temptation of the devil's money year after year. Yer gonna be mine to torture forever, ya hear?"*

Luke was wrong. He had to be wrong. Dear Lord, please make him be wrong. Nelda stumbled toward West Oakland, hacking as though her lungs turned themselves inside-out, the contents of her stomach bubbling and churning from the stink of a septic tank, Betty's burned flesh, and the sting of scorched dreams.

Laurel Anne Hill KOMENAR Publishing released *Heroes Arise*, Laurel Anne Hill's award-winning novel, in 2007. Her shorter works of fiction and nonfiction have appeared in a variety of publications, including *Spells and Swashbucklers*, *The Wickeds*, *A Bard's Eye View*, *Fault Zone*, and *Rum and Runestones*. HorrorAddicts.net voted Laurel Most Wicked 2011 for her steampunk/horror podcast, "Flight of Destiny." For more information on Laurel, go to:

laurelannehill.com

DARKNESS
by Dan Shaurette
Mount Tambora Volcanic Eruption in Indonesia, 1815

5 April 1815, evening
Sangir, Sumbawa, Dutch East Indies

What I mistook initially for the sound of cannon fire took my attention from my research. As I searched my memory to recall if I had seen such artillery in the port at Bima, the earth rumbled and our encampment rattled with vigour. Was our camp under fire?

"Gordon, what was that? Do you think that was Mount Marapi?" asked my wife Jenny.

"I'm not sure, my love, but I do know you shouldn't even be out of bed," I chided.

"Blame this child of ours who kicked me about the same time as the noise we heard."

"It sounded like a cannonade," said Nicolaas, my assistant.

I agreed, but Jenny added, "If that was cannon fire, the shake we felt would put impact right above us." For a lady who never saw combat, she had an eerie sense about such things. I had to admit she was correct.

"Nonetheless," I said. "I doubt that was Marapi. Perhaps it was Gunung Kelut or Bromo. Nicolaas and I will keep an eye out on the volcanoes. You should be back in bed."

She pouted as she made her way back to our makeshift bedroom. "I shall have my pad and pencils with me just in case."

Jenny is a talented artist, quite adept at capturing the savage beauty of the islands she likes to call "The

Ring of Fire." This expedition was as much hers as it was mine.

Later in the evening as ash fell, we knew for sure one of the volcanoes released it, but still it was not clear as to which gave up this cloud. The sunset was crimson on the horizon. Surely the sailors in the bay shall have a fine day ahead. Were I a superstitious man, I might consider the bloody sky some form of omen.

10 April 1815, approximately 7 P.M.

Three reports in close succession. If we thought cannons were fired over our heads last week, then tonight I would have been sure I was standing next to our return fire with ears unmuffled. The earth shook with a fury greater than any I have ever experienced.

My darling Jenny came running into my office, out of breath, the poor dear. "Gordon, Tambora has blown! Come quickly."

I should never have brought her on our expedition to Sumbawa, but her curiosity and stubbornness rivals even mine. Clearly this is why I love her so.

Grabbing my journal and pencil, I left the rest of my paperwork in a heap as I dashed to follow her outside. Jenny had already begun sketching when I caught up to her.

Never before had I seen such a thing. Mount Tambora had erupted three years ago by some reports, but only some smoke was seen from the peaks then. I dare say it is obvious last week's ash fall was also from Tambora.

Tambora's peak had until now been majestic in size, ranging at about two and a half miles. Tonight, I dare say half the mountain is gone, and three bright fountains of fire make up the rest, reaching heavenward as if to mock the sky.

We were in grave danger and made our way to evacuate at once.

Nicolaas attempted to gather our paperwork while I immediately urged Jenny to cease drawing long enough to gather up her pad, our pencils, my journal, and spyglass. Nothing but our safety was my concern, but whatever documentation we could carry of today's catastrophe, we took.

Once we arrived at Bima Bay, we found ourselves waiting with many natives for boats to escape the island. The ash was thick and airborne stones were also falling down, but in the darkness of night we could not tell from where it was all coming.

A gale picked up and made everything unbearable to witness. All of the papers Nicolaas carried were lost to us. I still have my journal, and Jenny has her pad. We alone shall continue to document the horror.

Jenny was rushed to the head of a line for a boat. However, she refused to board any vessel without me. I all but commanded her to take refuge, for herself and our unborn child. She would not obey me, and furthermore, she kept sketching while we waited. Remarkable woman, she actually smeared the ash that fell all around us onto her drawings, and from what I could see through the mess, it was a wholly accurate depiction of the chaos.

Eventually, a ship came close enough to the bay for us take a boat out to it. I was in one boat with Jenny, while Nicolaas took another boat with other refugees. To this day I shall thank my time rowing against my classmate John Polidori for the practice I needed to rush us out to catch the ship. Without hesitation, the ship's commander gave us permission to come aboard.

11 April 1815

The darkness of night has not fled to the break of dawn. Truly, the massive ash and rock ejected into the air overnight persists into an utterly black day.

What I have to share now breaks my heart for I no longer know what to do. Jenny has sketched the most horrific looking creature. Most disturbing of its visage is the red of the eyes and mouth. That was when I noticed the blood on her.

I immediately asked the captain if there was a doctor on board. He told me there was and that he was on his way to the island to offer aid and supplies. His name is Doctor Dirk Ambrosius, an ancient Dutchman to be sure. He seemed spry enough for his age, and intellect shone bright in his eyes. Whether it be an affectation or not, he set me at ease once I met him and brought him to Jenny.

12 April 1815

Dr. Ambrosius is here again and his news is the gravest. Poor Jenny has miscarried to a stillbirth. Naturally she is hysterical, but I am doing what I can to calm her. The good doctor has treated her with laudanum. He is concerned by the blood loss and is doing everything he can to prevent it.

Once she had fallen asleep, her breathing terribly shallow, I picked up Jenny's sketch pad again. The first few pages are of the glorious island I remember vividly, but now sadly can only be revisited by her artwork. I know it is daytime, but the darkness outside the ship is ever-present.

A stark change is seen also in Jenny's sketches as I flip through more of them. The remaining pages are almost solid black. Such horrible darkness, but in the lamplight I see eyes in the mad patterns of the sketch.

13 April 1815

She's dead. My beloved Jenny is dead. Dr. Ambrosius was unable to stop her bleeding after the birth.

I cannot stay in our cabin. Dr. Ambrosius let me take rest in his quarters while he tended to her remains. Before I went there, I went by to tell Nicolaas.

When I found Nicolaas in his cabin, he was drunk as sin, sitting at a small table with an empty glass. The smell of rum was all about him. I told him about Jenny, and he gave me the oddest expression before he offered his condolences. As I began to weep, for I could no longer contain my emotions, rather than console me, he began to berate me. Me!

"This is your fault, all of it!" he slurred. Clearly this was the alcohol talking, but when I asked him to explain, he seemed to sober up and said, "I, eh, mean this damned expedition and all of our research lost to Tambora's fury."

"And what about my beloved Jenny, and our child. I suppose I am to blame for their deaths. Clearly I made the island gods angry and—"

He stared at me as if by will alone he could bore through my soul. The most pained look took over his face, and in a motion I could not anticipate, he stood up, staggered, and punched me square in the face.

"I loved her too, you fool! Jenny and her child were—" he started but was interrupted as the ship lurched. He came forward and slipped, falling chin first into the side of the table where he was moments before sitting.

Even though he struck me, and even though his intentions were patently illicit, I still bent down to help him up. One night of drunken stupidity cannot erase years of friendship. At least such was the instinct I had. He on the other hand spit blood at me and told me to leave. Angrily, I turned and left his cabin, slamming his door shut behind me.

This cursed darkness is everywhere around us. Wet ash falls like rain, making the decks slippery. I could not find my way, and the scant few lanterns do little to cut through the night or day that seems as night.

Eventually I made my way to Dr. Ambrosius' quarters. I knocked and heard him shout, "Enter, young Gordon!"

Once inside, I found he had lit two lanterns, which thankfully provided some desperately needed light as he rummaged through his belongings.

"The captain brought a cot for you, young Gordon. If you still wish to sleep here tonight, I will not mind, so long as you can withstand my snoring, ya?" he said almost with a laugh in his voice. He pulled two thin red ribbons out of his luggage. Solemnly he tied one around a leg of my cot and the other to the leg of his bed.

Unfamiliar with the custom, I was about to ask him about it, but he anticipated this and said only, "Is tradition, you see? Don't worry on it." From a separate bag, he pulled out what looked to me in the dim light as pins or nails and a beaded necklace. I decided I should not bother to ask and took off my outer clothes which were filthy with muddy ash.

He took this as a hint and said, "You get comfortable, ya? I will be back." He bowed to me, and I nodded in kind. He took one of the lanterns and left the cabin. I went to bed shortly afterward, leaving the lantern on, for I did not want to sleep in the dark.

14 April 1815, morning

First Jenny and now Nicolaas is dead. No explanations have I to give. I went around to see him this morning. At least I believe it was morning. I've not been able to get any sleep, and it is always dark as night outside. When I knocked on his door, he did not answer.

The door was locked, so I made my way around to a window with a lantern. What I saw has shattered what little remains of my sanity. Blood coated the window so thick I could not see through, but beneath the light of the lamp, the red liquid was undeniable.

I called immediately for a deckhand to unlock the door. When he did so, we both recoiled at the stench and sight of the gore. Nicolaas was there, naked in bed, bathed in his own blood and organs ripped from his body.

The deckhand ran screaming from the room to get the captain, the doctor, and anyone else awake. As the boat pitched, I fell into the gore and cursed as all of my emotions from the past few days finally erupted from me like the hell that raged around us from Tambora.

"*Kuntilanak!*" came the shouts outside the cabin from more than one bystander.

Eventually the crowd parted, and the doctor walked in. He extended a hand to me and helped me up. Exhausted and slipping on the floor, I collapsed into him. As I did so, trying to regain my footing, he whispered to me, "Jenny, she is gone."

My ears must have deceived me, but as I was about to ask him to repeat what he said, a terrible shriek assaulted our ears from outside the cabin. Again the men shouted, "*Kuntilanak!*"

The captain calmed his men down and sent them all away with commands I did not understand. He approached the doctor and me with a grave expression and said, "I am sorry for your loss. Doctor, explain to him, while we search, yes?" The doctor nodded, and the captain left us alone with what was left of Nicolaas.

"You sit," he said as he pointed me to a chair, "while I examine."

"If you'll forgive me, Doctor, there's not a bloody lot left to examine," I said sharply.

As he delicately examined Nicolaas' body, he added, "Indeed, but beyond the obvious gore, it would seem he was mauled by something with very sharp claws. Something that was either very angry, very hungry, or quite possibly both."

Horrified, I only asked, "By what?"

That was when he looked away from Nicolaas and stared at me with the same examining gaze. "You would not believe me if I told you, young Gordon."

"Don't patronize me, Doctor. All of the death aboard this ship weakens my patience."

"Very well, the name the men shouted, *kuntilanak*, is a local legend of the islands. I heard the stories for many years when I worked here for the VOC. They say it is a monster that feasts on the blood of men, tearing them apart just as Nicolaas here can attest."

I was shocked! This supposed man of science was telling me superstitions and fairy tales. "What kind of monster exactly? Some kind of sea creature, perhaps?"

"Oh no, this is a creature that should be dead but refuses to die!"

"What do you mean, like a ghost?"

"No, no, the corpse is animated. *Kunti* are very specific though in how they are created and how they can be truly killed," he said with a very defeated sigh.

"And that is?"

"They are women who have died in childbirth," he began, but I interrupted him.

"Now wait just one minute. Do you mean to tell me..." I couldn't fathom what he proposed.

"Yes, your beautiful wife Jenny is now a savage *kuntilanak*, and she must be found and destroyed before she kills again."

14 April 1815, evening

The horror of the past few days has led to this. The captain commanded his crew to join the doctor and me as we searched the ship. Some of the other refugees have also joined us. We searched through the blasted darkness of yet another day, and I am exhausted as I report we have not found Jenny. Personally I fear some superstitious bastard has thrown my beloved's body overboard, but none have confessed to such notorious an action. I no longer know what to believe.

Dr. Ambrosius had gone to bed, and I laid in my cot failing miserably to get any rest. I could not fathom how he could sleep, but his snoring made it nearly impossible for me to do so. I put out the light and made another effort of it.

A loud scratching at our door awakened me. This was followed by a pounding that finally stirred Dr. Ambrosius. Before either of us could light a lantern, the door burst open and startled me as a blast of cold sea air rushed in and filled the room. I fell out of my cot. Shadows moved towards me, and I saw unbearably bright eyes like flames, open and staring at me hungrily.

Dr. Ambrosius shouted something at the shadows in Dutch. I did not understand, but clearly the shadow did, for it backed away from me slowly, warily. Ambrosius grabbed something from his bag near his bed, neither without leaving the bed nor without looking away from the shadowy creature. He leapt at the creature but tumbled as he tangled in his bed sheets.

Something metallic dropped to the floor and a great shriek came from the creature. It slashed at the doctor, and he screamed in pain as he was torn to pieces in the darkness before me. I staggered back into my cot and screamed, "Stop it, damn you! Jenny! Stop!"

To my shock, the slashing stopped, and with a new shriek, this time almost forlorn, it ran out the door and into the darkness beyond. Quickly I lit a lantern and once it was alight I wished I hadn't as I saw the doctor on the floor, his chest and torso bloody and gored. The doctor was gasping, gurgling up blood, but was able to point to a corner of his bed. In the light I could see a large iron nail. I grabbed it, and he said with great difficulty, "You must... you must do this. Her neck, young Gordon." With that, he exhaled and expired.

I pulled myself together and sat upright in my cot. As I began to consider what I was meant to do, I looked up, and there stood Jenny. At least I thought it was her. Her long blond hair was black as midnight, and she was naked and pale even in the dim light of the lantern. Wisps of some kind of cloth clung to her and flowed around her in a breeze I could not feel. It was even colder in the room, and I could see my breath, but none from her.

She stared at me. Her once beautiful blue eyes were bloodshot with enormous pupils dilated beyond their normal size. Bloody tears ran down her ashen face. She didn't say a word, but I could tell she was tormented by what she had done. Her expression pleaded with me, but if it was for forgiveness or peace, I could not know.

I looked down at the nail in my hand, and I did not know what I was meant to do. Did Ambrosius actually have this, wielding it against her? I tossed the strange weapon away to roll around uselessly on the floor by the bedside table where I had left Jenny's sketch pad.

She smiled at me and pointed at the pad, wanting me to see it. Wanting to show me something. She didn't speak. Perhaps she couldn't speak and wanted to communicate with me through the pad. I nodded and left the cot. As I turned away from her for the slightest moment, I heard her shriek.

I looked back to her and saw her eyes, nose, and mouth blaze, bright as the flames from Tambora, and then she crumbled to ash before my eyes, revealing the ship's captain behind her, wielding another large iron nail.

I stood there dumbfounded as the captain sighed with tormented relief on his grim face. The darkness of midnight which plagued us these last few days had finally broken to grey and slowly brightening patches of purple and orange.

A brief wind entered the cabin, slowly blowing away the ashes where my beloved Jenny once stood. No, that hadn't been Jenny, not anymore. At least she had peace, and the time has come for me to find some as well.

Dan Shaurette has been a goth-geek and horror addict—especially of vampires—ever since seeing Bela Lugosi's *Dracula* as a child. He recently produced a podcast version of his vampire novel, *Lilith's Love*, and also hosts the *Out Of The Coffin* podcast. To find out more about Dan, go to:

DanShaurette.com

WINTER OF TERROR
by H. E. Roulo
Avalanches of Austria-Switzerland, 1950-51

Skis hissed across ice, alerting the creature that something new came to its mountain. The small beast crept from a dark tunnel, blinking and sniffing. This winter was the hardest in memory. The nearest small village remained snowed in, blocked from contact with the outside world. Yet a skier swished by, wrapped up against the cold. He traveled alone, with worn gear and only a backpack to hold his possessions. His actions either said he didn't care what happened to him or he could take care of himself. Either way, this was a new element to work with and a fleeting opportunity. Icicle-tipped fingers scrabbled against the icy crust of snow, as if figuring a difficult math problem. With narrowed eyes, it plotted.

Unaware of his inhuman audience, Lukas paused, heart pounding. Gleaming snow mounded the cornice of the mountain where it hovered like a frozen wave. The path to his objective led straight underneath—if the alpine village really existed. He was starting to doubt it as much as the stories of dangerous creatures. He was a sucker for a mystery, and those tales had turned this bum toward the town of misfortune.

The faded military-green canvas backpack he wore pinched his shoulder. He jerked a strap tight, reflecting how five years after his service, it still held up. Better than he had, actually, considering they had wandered the same back roads. When the war ended, he'd thought his path would lead back home, but it never did. Maybe it never could. Home held warm remembrances of soft people. Lukas was so hard he'd be like a razor blade tearing through the place.

Growling at memories time and loneliness still hadn't stripped clean, he pulled off a wool mitten to shove up goggles and wipe his forehead. Ice gleamed like a knife poised to drop. The smart thing would be to go around, maybe find a ridge.

Exposure to wind and reflected sunlight had darkened his cheeks and forehead. Lukas squinted. Pale creases flared from the corners of his eyes. No one would mistake them for smile lines—more like the stripes of a jungle predator. He strapped goggles back into place over rough skin. When had he ever done the smart thing?

With a hiss, his skis pushed off once more, their rasp breaking the hushed silence. He'd learned no matter where you were, the world could collapse without caring you were standing right underneath.

Lukas swished around the lee of the mountain. Thirty pointy-roofed buildings, a church, and herds of goats lay nestled in the foothills like a scene out of a child's snow globe. Wisps of gray smoke, too far away to smell, promised fire for his toes. He admired the stillness, as if time and life had frozen solid in the cold and would reawaken in the summer. He gave thanks that it was a real place. He sure would have hated to freeze to death over a rumor. Perhaps the other, darker tales, creeping in whispers to the world outside, were true as well, Grimm's-like sugar-coated tales of calamity. They told stories of monsters and lost children.

A drift of fine snow crystals whipped against Lukas's face. He blinked. Had something just scampered across the icy ledge? His ski poles moved faster. The hillside underneath him shook as if under the rapid thud of large feet. Protection didn't exist on the bare white field; just more speed instinct told him wouldn't be enough.

Breaking ice exploded onto the quiet hillside.

Sharp crystals, rocks, and broken tree limbs flooded the slope, sweeping Lukas off his skis. Gasping mouthfuls of air as sky whipped past, he pulled his arms to his chest and covered his face with both hands. Rolling with the small avalanche brought him to the edge of the tumbling debris. Trapped.

Friction-warmed crystals refroze, bonding together like concrete around his battered body. Cold on every side, bruised and buried, he panted into the dark unable to move his jaw enough to curse aloud. Snow coated him like the finest plaster mold. If he were made of marble, pale and white and cool, he could be shipped safely to the farthest corner of the world. Except, of course, he was already there.

The tiny air pocket above his nose filled with his warm exhalations, reminding him of childhood. When monsters crept through his dark room, he'd pulled his blankets above his tousled head and stayed under there until the air reeked of childish breath and sweat rolled along his spiky hairline. He'd burst out for a quick breath and a glimpse of the creeping things living behind his closet door, never certain what he'd seen.

What was that thing on the hillside?

The kid was long gone, and what covered him weren't blankets he could just push aside. Snow walls closed around him. His lip quivered. He sucked in a shallow breath. The stale air ensured he wouldn't suffer too long. Half an hour, maximum. Not too long to fight, he figured, and he'd make the moments count. If the end came after so short a time, there would be no shame in it. It would be a quiet death, which was more than he'd expected. His jaw firmed.

He tried to sit up but nothing budged. When he wiggled, the weight of snow held his legs tight. The arm he'd lifted to protect his face was still trapped over him. He carefully flicked a finger on his raised hand. Snow trickled down, coating his nose and upper lip. He snorted, clearing his nostrils. Though it might make his situation worse, he had to try something. A moment passed while he considered the real possibility of suffocation. Then, with a big breath in, he punched. Ice poured onto his face. His head jerked, mouth filling with curses that couldn't get out. His hand, only inches above, angled around an armful of snow as he scraped his nose free. Cool air whispered across his lips, fresh and filled with the pungent tang of broken evergreen trees. He'd been lucky. His face had been barely buried.

"Stay back!" a voice hissed in cruel tones.

Doubting his ears, Lukas's numb fingers shoved ice to free his jaw. He'd lost a mitten. "Is someone there? I'm here!"

Real enough, a man asked, "You survived?"

"Well, it's not the dead talking!" Lukas bit back a curse. "I'm almost free. Help dig me out."

"Dig you out. Yes, of course. Help is here. I will dig you out."

Someone stomped around. Lukas swiped until he'd uncovered most of his face. A man, dressed in the local garb and muffled to his nose against the snow, scooted across the ice with a heavy branch. The stranger's head twitched as he crept across the icy field, shoulders raised to his ears. Lukas wondered what could make the man so afraid. And slow. Was he delaying in case there was another avalanche? The man edged around his head, just out of sight.

Lukas gritted his teeth. "Well?"

Something hard rammed his shoulder, and Lukas screamed. He wrenched upright, grabbed his shoulder, and glared at the man who cowered back.

Both of them were surprised Lukas had been able to rip himself free of the snow's cold grasp.

"Sorry, sorry, I went too fast."

"Are you trying to kill me?" Lukas groaned. The man knelt, still holding the limb he'd driven into Lukas. Lukas examined the ripped fabric over his shoulder, seeing a long scrape in the skin. "You about tore my shoulder open."

At Lukas's tone, the man nibbled on his dirty white mustache, sitting back on his heels. His gaze flickered, not meeting Lukas's eyes for more than a heartbeat.

"I hurried to know how many in your party."

Lukas squinted at the man, doubting it. "Just me."

His legs had been buried in deeper drifts so Lukas used the branch to chip away at snow and ice. The man helped lift cold heavy blocks.

"Just you," the man said as if rebuking himself.

Engaged in freeing body parts, Lukas didn't take time to glance up. The skin behind his ears crawled, probably from melting snow, but the closeness of the muttering man didn't help his nerves.

"But they know you're up here? You're from the village?"

Lukas, jerked free his left foot and pulled to release his right. "Do I look like I'm from around here?"

"No?"

The man's uncertainty added to Lukas's irritation. Was he uncertain or just uncertain what to make of Lukas? He didn't give off an air of respectability, it was true, but neither did his would-be rescuer. Lukas grimaced, unable to regret his sharpness. He'd freed both legs, and a familiar prickle raced down his spine. He'd left the army on a long

115

walk, and surviving that walk meant listening to his instincts. They screamed wrongness, but what kind?

He studied the man from the corner of his eye, muscles tight as he levered himself to his feet. Big man had crazy eyes that never stopped moving. Guilty eyes. Ignoring the man's outstretched hands, Lukas tested his injured shoulder, lips turning white. A few quick twirls of his uninjured arm had his scarf off, but he couldn't figure out how to knot it one-handed to form a sling for his arm.

"I will help," a new voice offered, so hesitant a strong breeze might have been making the words.

Crazy Eyes jerked straight and glared at a soft-voiced boy who shuffled closer. Little more than eight or nine, the kid's weight hardly broke the crust of snow. He possessed vivid blue eyes and hair as white as the snow sticking to his knitted cap. The scarf slipped through Lukas's mittened hand. Though he'd never have let Crazy Eyes assist him, he let the boy gather the soft cloth.

Lukas sensed tension between the two of them. The man's hands clenched, seeking an excuse to snatch the boy away. Rather than satisfy Crazy Eyes by refusing the boy, Lukas bit his tongue and steeled himself when the boy touched his neck while tying the scarf into place. Gingerly, Lukas slid his arm into the improvised sling.

"Thanks, kid. Both of you. I didn't think I'd get out of that one."

"I'm sorry," the boy apologized, turning paler.

Crazy Eyes flicked a look between them, as if resenting each word the boy spent on Lukas.

"What for, sport?" Lukas asked. Throw a baseball cap on him and he'd fit right into the neighborhood back home, except for his haunted eyes and thick layer of dirt. You could tell at a glance he'd

116

smell bad in warmer weather. These weren't goat-milk-fattened alpine herders. They were something else, something strange.

"I'm Lukas. You all have names?"

The child stilled, like a deer sensing hunters. His eyes flickered to Crazy Eyes, who stomped toward them in the snow.

"You are a stranger. Leave. The village is that way."

"Well, now." Lukas squinted, the tiger stripes at the corners of his eyes hidden. "I'm weary and soaked to the bone. You have a cabin up here?"

Involuntarily, the boy glanced up the slope.

Lukas could use a fire and time to wrap his shoulder. Bruises could hurt this bad, he knew, and prayed it wasn't anything worse thanks to the old man's clumsiness. After his mauling the least the man could do was invite Lukas to sit by the fire. By his reasoning, the polite thing to do was ignore the man's bad manners. Lukas asked himself, "Would I like to come in? Do I plan to survive today's adventure? Don't mind if I do."

Disregarding the sputtering man, Lukas used the tree limb like a ski pole to help him uphill. His skis were long gone, lost beneath furrowed heaps of snow. His backpack had stayed attached, or he'd have been without worldly possessions, small as they were. Of course, it didn't matter how far he walked, the memories just came along. Sighing, Lukas hitched the bag higher. He bit back an oath when his shoulder protested. His strides increased, since he wanted to get this over with.

Lukas's sudden decision to find their cabin startled something in the brush. An unseen animal scrambled along the remaining tree line, whistling like a marmot and clicking like tumbling icicles. Lukas plowed into the bushes, determined to see what made such a ruckus. Strange tracks marked the snow. He stared, mumbling. The prints looked like big bare feet.

The kid came to his side and peered down.

"What's that all about, Jimmy?" he asked.

Surprised at the new name, pink flooded Jimmy's cheeks along with a shy grin. His pleasure paled under Crazy Eyes's glare.

"Lies," Crazy Eyes snarled. "The boy leaves tracks to trick us." He reached around Lukas to strike Jimmy, the open handed blow staggering the boy and destroying the prints.

Lukas shoved, realizing how big the man was and how weak he'd become from being trapped and nearly frozen. Still, the shove distracted Crazy Eyes from the boy. He raised his eyebrows in shock, mouth clamped shut.

Mentally, Lukas dubbed him Nils. Better to call him a common name than slip up. Though the name Crazy Eyes was so apt, Nils would probably answer to it before he realized the insult.

Lukas smirked at his private joke, making Nils stomp from foot to foot as Lukas helped Jimmy up.

"Tell me more lies, kid," Lukas invited.

Jimmy's teeth chattered as he peered at Nils, but the man ignored him. Jimmy took silence for permission. They continued their climb toward the cabin with Nils trailing behind.

"There's a barbegazi. It follows us." Seeing Lukas's raised eyebrow, he raced backward alongside Lukas to tell his fable. "Barbegazi live in these hills, sleeping in summer. They're kind of like gnomes, but all icicled and with big feet for skiing over avalanches. That's their good fun. This one's gotta be having a wonderful time this winter." His voice trailed off with an envious sigh.

Lukas flexed his hands, wishing he hadn't lost a mitten. Over his shoulder, he could see anger radiated like heat off Nils. The man liked his privacy. Nothing wrong with that. Lukas knew he shouldn't judge so harshly off looks and a bad feeling. After all, he could imagine how he looked at the moment. Still, the twitch in the back of his neck, as if he could feel Nils glaring, wouldn't go away.

Done arguing with himself, since it hadn't made him or Nils any prettier, he turned his attention to the cabin in the distance. Little more than a shepherd's summer shack, the day's fading light gleamed through chinks in the thick gray boards.

"Barbegazi set off avalanches." Spit froze on Nils's lips, hardening like his words about the creature whose existence he'd already denied.

"They don't. They ride them!" Jimmy shouted.

Nils's face turned red.

Jimmy cowered.

Acid burned in the back of Lukas's throat. What kind of life could this kid have with a dad like that?

"I'm too big for children's tales." Lukas said, laughing to relieve the strain between them. His gaze returned to his goal. Inside the cabin he could sort this thing out—once his hands weren't blocks of ice and his feet lead weights. A step into deeper snow and the tree limb pole slipped from his clumsy fingers.

Jimmy took off his hat, shaking ice away, slipped it over Lukas's free hand, and placed his own mittened hand around it to hold it there. Hand-in-hand, they trod a few steps more. Rather than help, the boy exerted pressure to slow him.

"My parents said barbegazi dig through snow with their feet. They're big, like snowshoes." He

119

panted, sweaty, as if his myths were dangerous. "My parents said they'd help if you were in trouble."

"Where are your parents, kiddo?" Lukas asked in an undertone.

A marmot hooted warning.

As if shot, Jimmy fell, dragging Lukas with him. A tree limb slammed through the space where Lukas's head had been. He rolled, favoring his shoulder, and bounded to his feet. In Nils's crazy eyes he read his own death. His spine lit up with terror and adrenaline surged like a familiar tune.

Nils howled and kicked the boy who cowered at his feet. Jimmy's slender body flew through the air, landing on a stump with a loud crack.

Cursing, Lukas charged Nils.

Nils lowered his shaggy head like a mountain goat and slammed into Lukas's bad shoulder. Pain flared red across Lukas's vision. Helpless, he slid across the tumbled field with Nils paces away. His senses swam as the larger man stomped closer. Where was Jimmy? All Lukas could think was he needed to keep the other man's focus. He had to distract him from the injured boy. Groggy, Lukas threw snow and scrambled backward to the stump, keeping himself between them.

The snow lay empty and wrapped smoothly around the stump. Jimmy had disappeared into the white field, as if he'd sunk into the snow never to reappear. Nils swept his rolling gaze around to return to Lukas where he stood gasping in the snow, shoulder hanging.

"Where's he gone? You came to steal him from me!" Nils scrambled to the stump, clawing at the snow as if Jimmy were his most prized possession. Lukas didn't know how Jimmy had done it, but it seemed obvious the kid wasn't going to suddenly show up again.

Nils cooed the boy's name, forgetting he'd just gotten done kicking Jimmy for speaking to Lukas. The man's madness sent shivers through Lukas. Gritting his teeth at the image of the frightened boy's life with the crazy hermit on the mountain, Lukas dashed to the cabin and tore open the door, gagging at the stench inside.

War was better than this.

A goat burst past him, onto the hillside. Butchered carcasses lay in a corner among goat droppings. A bed in one corner, a pallet of rags in the other, and a strange collection of bits and pieces bespoke the man's madness. Ropes were everywhere, as if he penned more than goats in the cabin when he could find victims. Lukas swallowed his gorge and entered. As cold as outside and worse smelling, inside the cabin he found what he sought. A small hatchet rested above the fireplace out of a child's reach. Lifting it, he turned back to the door.

"Get out of my home," Nils boomed.

"How long have you had the boy?"

"He's mine!"

"You kidnapped him!"

"He stays. You've seen it. He could run off, but he doesn't."

"Because you tell him you'd hunt him down and kill him. Or maybe you tell him you'd kill his parents, right?"

Nils's eyes gleamed, steady but no less mad. "I tell him I'll bury the village. I know where the snowpack is thickest." The big man quivered, cackled, and shoved the door shut. Lukas threw himself against the door, but nothing budged. Outside, the man muttered and cursed, occasionally calling out to the boy as he worked. Black smoke, heavy and slow, wafted through a crack. More followed, billowing to the roof.

"You demanded my hospitality? Enjoy it! Fire and shelter! Meat and bone!" The words became a fading sing-song.

Lying on the floor to avoid the worst smoke, Lukas belly-crawled to the wall. Fire burned in the moss between boards, catching and searing into the bigger logs. He found a spot where it hadn't caught and used his hatchet, wishing he had the use of both arms. The cracks of his blows echoed, and he despaired. If Nils got it into his crazy brain to stop Lukas, he could do it. The hatchet would be easy to grab away or the fire redirected into the ragged hole.

But Nils didn't return.

Because Nils means to release an avalanche on the village. And poor Jimmy, finally free, was headed there now. Lukas tried to still his imagination, but thoughts surged with each strike of his hatchet. Jimmy would be the first victim as snow crashed down the slope. Buildings could be smashed to smithereens by the shockwave traveling ahead of snow. What would it do to a small boy's body? The papers were full of other recent tragedies, where avalanches destroyed forests, smothered herds of animals, and buried villages. One village had been hit with six avalanches in under an hour.

The one that hit Lukas had been small, and just thinking about it terrified him.

Wood flew under Lukas's blows. The hatchet bit again and again. Fire crackled through the walls, filling the space until he sweated and coughed black air. The log splintered. Lowering his head, he fought the blackness biting at the edge of his vision. The heavy hatchet fell from his grip.

Earlier today he'd thought he'd fall asleep in ice and cold, but it looked like it was to be heat and fire after all. He'd seen men like him die screaming, and told himself he wouldn't be surprised. Yet he was. He didn't want to go this way. His eyes drifted to the small hole he'd made, where the log bent back. The wood shifted, and gray smoke swirled over the floor of the cabin as fresh air rushed in. Icy fingers, dripping like tears, pried at the log.

More air entered, brisk and clean. Panting, Lukas brought his legs around and kicked the wall. The impact flung a soft body on the outside back into the snow. It hooted weakly.

Lukas pressed himself into the hole, screaming when his injured shoulder caught and dragged against the edge. The ragged wood scraped off his green canvas backpack as he wiggled free. Cursing, he yanked at the black and smoking canvas bag, gasping at the heat of fire pressing toward him. Blisters appeared on his knuckles, but he couldn't let go. With a ripping sound, the bag tore free. Lukas staggered. The corner of his uniform, taken off the day he deserted but never left behind, sizzled against the snow. He scooped it up, fire and ice together, shoved it back inside and yanked the cords shut.

Crying with the pain of slipping the strap over his bad shoulder, Lukas fell into the snow and held himself there, the coolness soothing blisters on his hands, cheeks, and shoulders. Behind him, the thatched roof collapsed in a storm of sparks.

Night had fallen. He blinked and looked away from the bonfire cleansing an evil house. The fading afterimage of fire lay superimposed over a small figure staggering toward him.

"Jimmy?" Lukas stumbled forward to meet him, falling. Coughs shook his body. "He's gone to set off the avalanche. We have to stop him."

"He's on the *snow* now," Jimmy said, as if that meant something important.

"But—" Lukas blinked, wavering on his knees. It looked almost as if the snow swarmed with tiny figures, each boulder of snow a pointed hat above icicle beards and green gleaming eyes.

"Can you see the serac? It's there, layers of ice and snow piled four stories high at the edge of the glacier." The child's weak voice exalted and then faded with a whimper. "He thinks he can get above it, but he can't. They'll get there first."

"I can't see anything. It's too dark outside the fire." He wrapped his arms around Jimmy.

The kid shivered, though the fire burned against Lukas's back even through his backpack and heavy coat. Flames crackled angrily. He lifted the boy, who didn't notice, just moaned.

"Jimmy, you okay?"

"You saved me from him."

Lukas wasn't so sure. He touched the cold hands, feeling along the curved body. The child groaned when he pressed his stomach. "I think he injured you when he kicked you."

"That's old." The child gasped. "I always recover. I'm tough, he says. I lasted the longest."

Solemnly, the child swiped cold fingers along Lukas's rough cheek. "The barbegazi saved me when they could."

Cursing, Lukas crouched over the child. His injured arm made carrying the boy any further impossible.

"What's your name, son?" Tears traveled the pale channels beside his eyes. The boy peered above his shoulder, at the invisible serac hidden in the night. Lukas said, "We-we'll need to find the right family."

"I'm all that's left of the ones he took. Jan and Hans, and Anders and the two Saras." The boy's voice whispered as quietly as falling snow. "Tell them we wanted to come home but didn't know we could."

Inside his arms, the boy heaved a sigh and relaxed, the spark in his eyes fading to green then gone. Just as softly, the mountain heaved a great sigh and released its cover of snow. The tide flooded down the slope. Shapes soared across the ice, as if skiing, leaping across trees and over boulders, and herded the ravenous snow toward the cabin.

Huddled over the boy's body as the snow engulfed their small ravine, Lukas panted with memories of suffocation. "Please, God, no. I want to live."

The burning cabin burst apart. Boards soared upward as if reaching for escape, but jagged ice and smashing snow swallowed the debris, smothering every ember with an angry roar. The mountain groaned, cleansed of its hillside infection.

The tide lifted Lukas and tore Jimmy from his weak grasp. Debris smashed into the side of his head, sending a spark across his vision and then the blackness of burial.

Lukas returned to consciousness clutching at snow. He gasped, clawing in the darkness. His flailing arms found a ragged tunnel, as if scratched out by icicle-tipped fingers. He crawled along the escape route. Snow collapsed the tunnel behind him with hushed whomps, like a slow heartbeat.

Nils's body, crushed and battered, lay atop a smooth flow. His crazy eyes were clouded by death, and his mouth hung open in astonishment.

Lukas searched, but found no sign of Jimmy's body. Just his own backpack, empty of all the burdens he'd carried across the Alps.

The avalanche of tumbling ice and debris had taken the two men most of the way down the hillside. Despite the avalanche flowing almost to their doors, the village lay untouched. Lukas wasn't surprised. After all, these people had already suffered enough. The barbegazi, and the mountain they served, had ensured that no more children would disappear this winter. For this tiny town, the Winter of Terror *ended* with an avalanche.

Lights moved in a line on the hillside below as villagers crept from their homes to investigate the slide. Soon they'd arrive, full of questions and solicitation. They'd take him down the mountain.

In a moment, beside a warm fire, he'd have to tell them about brave Jimmy and fate of the other children unwillingly stolen away. The families would be sad, but grateful to have answers.

Lukas folded the worn green canvas cloth underneath him as he sat under the twinkling sky, listening to contented hoots from far across the mountain. He thought about going home. Home would be good.

H.E. Roulo's science-fiction novel *Fractured Horizon* is available as a downloadable audiobook at Podiobooks.com. It was a 2009 Parsec Award Finalist for Best Speculative Fiction Story (novel). H.E. Roulo's short stories have appeared in several magazines and anthologies, including *The Wickeds* and the HorrorAddicts.net podcast. For more information about Heather, go to: heroulo.com

OREVWA
by Jennifer Rahn
Haitian Earthquake, 2010

The last drops of wine splashed out of Zoe's glass as it fell over, spreading like a blood stain across the white table cloth. She drunkenly reached out to set it to rights, only to have it roll farther from her grasp as her knuckles bumped against it.

Shouldn't let him get to me like that.

Two wine bottles stood empty, drained witnesses of her misery. The remainders of a chocolate cake lay in ruins across from them, having been mauled by Zoe grabbing fistfuls of it, which she must have eaten. Cheap little twisty candles poked helter-skelter out of the cake disaster, their white wicks untouched by fire. She didn't give a damn one way or another.

Happy fortieth, Zoe. May the rest of your life not suck quite as bad.

Things probably weren't going to improve, if she believed the fortune teller she'd visited yesterday. The nine of pentacles had stared at her woefully from the top of the Celtic cross. Didn't matter which deck had been used or how Zoe had tried to rephrase the question, the answer never changed. An independent woman. Alone in her luxury. No family to drain her wealth. Alone. Lonely.

He'd actually said, "I don't know how it makes you feel. How am I supposed to know if you don't tell me?" Playing the disingenuous fool who couldn't possibly imagine her reaction to seeing photos of him fondling another woman at what was supposed to be her birthday party. The surprise party—boy, was it ever!—he'd put together after cancelling the one she'd already set up, planning instead the event to which he'd invited mostly his own friends and ignored her. And he'd lied about a lot of things, like smoking and how he got drunk nearly every night, and liked to date his ex-wife and/or ex-girlfriends when Zoe worked late or was stuck at home sick. The topper, though, was when he'd said she lacked independence, and if she didn't change her behaviour, it would be over between them. *Goodbye, jerk.*

Lacked independence? She'd been alone for eleven years before him, and it looked like things weren't going to change. To her amazement she'd fancied herself in love with him. She'd ignored all of his other lies, wanting so badly to believe the one in which he'd said he wanted to get married. The last had led to her wasting an entire year of her life in hopeful expectation, when she could have been with someone else, someone who actually wanted what he said he wanted.

No such person existed, leaving her with only the nine of pentacles.

I need a vacation.

She'd heard Cuba was really nice. One of her cousins had been there last year or maybe the year before.

Feeling like the walking dead, Zoe shuffle-stumbled over to her computer and typed in a quick search for vacation packages. As she clicked through the various pages on Caribbean vacations, the idea of a holiday started to brighten her mood. An ad on the side of her web browser caught her eye.

Adopt from Haiti.

She paused, her mouse hovering over it. Surely the woman in the nine of pentacles could adopt if she wished. Bypass the whole stupid marriage thing.

Is that what you really want?

I don't really want to be alive right now.
May as well at least go on a trip, then.
Zoe pressed down on the left mouse button.

Christmas in Haiti. The idea had sounded crazy, but once Zoe was there, it was a pleasant distraction, all bright, musical, and festive, undaunted by the obvious poverty surrounding the celebrations. She felt detached from it, but in an okay way, not carrying the undertones of hostility she'd felt when she withdrew from her family's traditional Christmas free-for-all to come down here to beaches and complete strangers.

Her aunts and uncles all wanted to help, but it was like they wished to command her into happiness, rather than dig up the root of her discontent and plant something else to grow and fill the emptiness. They were all waiting impatiently for her return, causing her to obstinately extend her stay for another three weeks. After all, it had been their idea she think carefully about whether she really wanted to adopt, and what better place than in the country she was thinking of adopting from?

To be honest, though, all she had really done was mope on the beach or in the tiny hotel bar, putting off facing her reality, not really having the nerve or emotional stamina to follow up on the phone calls she'd already made to the orphanage. Rebellion had clouded her ideals and muddied her mind.

All around her the quaint buildings were fronted with happy façades built specially for tourists, and it all felt exactly as unreal as the rest of her life.

Slipping on a pair of sandals, Zoe summoned a spark of motivation and wandered away from her room at the Coconut Villa Hotel, letting the direction of the gentle sea-scented breeze guide her steps through the streets of Port-au-Prince. Part of her mind cautioned her not to wander too far from the populated main streets, but her soul simply yearned to be drawn by the natural forces. The warmth of the sun, the pulse of the beautiful Haitian people, the tides, or the grounding energy of the earth beckoned.

If she closed her eyes for a few steps as she walked, listened to the mixed chatter of French and Haitian Creole around her, and imagined she could feel the Earth spin, the deep funk she'd been mired in was drawn slowly, steadily out of her body. The banishment of negative energy definitely helped, but still didn't make her feel really, truly alive. A wave of heat rolled over her and made her stumble just as she passed a little coffee shop. Nausea reared its head. She stepped into the nearly empty cafe, looking for something to drink, anything cold to push back the heat. Completely drained, she sat at a little, white-washed table for two.

"You are in wrong seat, Ma'am."

Zoe opened her eyes to see a little girl fidgeting uncomfortably in front of her.

"Is for Boko Agwe. Don' sit there. Boko serves with both hands. His power can walk in both light and dark."

Boko? Wasn't that some sort of Haitian shaman? Had she accidentally offended a local magician?

A server came by with a tall glass of lemonade and shooed the child away. He distinctly put the glass on the table with only one hand, and the name on his tag read Jean-Baptiste.

Zoe sat up and tried to shake the cobwebs from her mind. She twisted around to see where the child had run outside, wanting to talk to her some more, perhaps make sense of what she'd just said. She heard a funny little pop and a sharp pain snapped through her neck, almost as if someone had given a hard tug on the necklace she wore.

"*Vle kèk bonbon, M'selle?*"

A little bewildered, Zoe turned back to the server and shook her head, refusing the candies he offered her. The motion seemed to make her depression slide around in her mind and spill away as if someone had snapped their fingers and lit a small ember somewhere deep in her core. The server gave her a warm smile, white teeth showing intensely in his dark face. He pointed at her throat.

"Is pretty, *M'selle*. Erzulie Mansur. Agwe speaks to her."

Zoe looked down, her fingers going to a small silver charm she had bought from a street vendor selling rosaries and jewellery featuring several Catholic saints. Utterly confused, she looked up from the small image of the Virgin Mary to see the server nodding to another man in the cafe before looking back at her knowingly.

"Oh, no. This is the Virgin Mary," she tried to explain.

Jean-Baptiste laughed. "Is just what you think, *M'selle*. Erzulie is the one who lives here. She is the great *loa* of creation. Of life. You wear this and you don't know?"

"And Agwe?"

The server chuckled again, leaned in a bit too close and winked. "Her lover. Named after the lord of the sea."

Zoe decided to smile and not pursue the conversation, feeling somewhat out of her depth. She sat for a while longer, sipping the lemonade, thinking she should take advantage of the break in her mood—since it might not last—and visit the orphanage. She had put it off for so long it was

131

January twelfth. She only had two more days to explore her options before going home.

The time was already four-thirty. Perhaps she would not be able to visit, but she could at least find out where the orphanage was and have a look at the buildings, one little pro-active step closer. Checking her map, she decided to catch a cab, since the Children's Hospital housing the facility was not really in walking distance, especially in this heat.

As she walked to the door, the waiter called to her, *"Orévwa, M'selle."*

"Au revoir," she replied, smiling at the sound of the word in Haitian Creole. She headed back towards the hotel, thinking it would be easiest to find a cab there.

The little girl from the cafe peered at her from an alleyway but seeing herself discovered, pulled back, her sandals striking the pavement as she ran. The sight of her tugged on Zoe's heart, encouraging her to find a child of her own. Still nicely warm on the inside, as opposed to just outside, Zoe felt herself actually smiling as she jogged over to peek down the alley. Perhaps she could tease the child into talking to her for a little while, but the alley was empty. Sighing her disappointment, she shrugged it off and continued on her way, back toward the hotel, enjoying the play of tropical light off the colourful sidings of the buildings along the street. It figured. She'd only begin to really relax when she was about to leave this eclectic bit of paradise.

A warm breeze lifted the hair from her face as she passed by a second side street, making her turn to look. A small wooden sign squeaked from its hinges in the wind, its weathered, illegible surface marking the opening of a shop. She strolled over to the window as though she hadn't been going somewhere only a moment ago. Various tapestries and statuettes depicting Catholic figures were displayed, along with skulls and rather tribal looking bowls and instruments. Their bright colours and careful placement piqued Zoe's curiosity, and despite her intention to face the looming issues in her mind, she decided to take a quick detour into the shop.

Little bells over the door announced her presence. As her eyes adjusted to the dimmer light inside, she saw several dark eyes turn to take in her pale skin. She smiled; they nodded, and went back to their French-sounding conversation.

The shop offered musical instruments, soap, clothing, what she gathered were vials of folk medicine, along with the strange mixture of Catholic and, well, not Catholic items. Stone skulls with embedded candles, little grass dolls, bone fragments, and modified saints with little white cards at their feet stating something about *Santeria* gazed back at her.

"You look to become Mama?" One of the girls tending the shop approached her, pointing at Zoe's necklace as the waiter had.

"Um. Hello. You're the second person to notice my necklace."

"Ah!" The girl chuckled. "You have light that wants speak to Erzulie Mansur. She is the protector of children."

Catholicism obviously had different layers to it here than it did at home. "I see. Strange that I should have picked this one."

"It's not strange. You want that, Madame? To be Mama? Many women do. Here. This will help you." The girl put a small stone necklace in Zoe's hand and reached over to take a bottle of gold-coloured liquid from the shelf. "This is also made for the same purpose." She paused, looking over Zoe's face

133

intently. "It is worrisome," she mused, "that your inner light is wavering."

Mildly disturbed by her comment, Zoe broke eye contact, pretending to be very interested on what sat on the shelves. A small bottle full of what looked like pink and silver sand caught her eye. Before she could reach out to take it, the girl gently touched her arm.

"Oh, not that one, Madame."

"That one should not be out!" An older woman bustled over and grabbed the vial. "Very sorry, Madame. Many things for you here, but not this."

"What is it?"

"Dis? Dis is nothing. *De rien!*" The woman laughed and waved her hand dismissively.

"Zombie dust," someone muttered.

Zoe turned but couldn't determine who had spoken. "For real? It looks like bath salt."

"Oh, no, not for bathing."

The world suddenly broke and slid sideways. For an instant Zoe thought it was the heat getting to her again, but the sensation didn't stop. The other people in the shop felt it too. Some of them managed to run out of the shaking shop and into the street, but through the front window, Zoe could clearly see it was no safer out there. The buildings lining the narrow streets crumbled to bits as they came crashing down with the force of the earthquake. The building across the street collapsed into itself as the earth shook and split. The front window shattered under the weight of the collapsing roof, and shards of glass and window frame blasted inwards, one of them hitting the older woman in the back, sending her sprawling.

The vial of silvery-pink powder flew from the shopkeeper's hand. It hit the shifting floor and bounced, spinning lazily as the cork lost its grip and went off in another direction. The vial ricocheted off the floor and the odd, glittery dust sailed into Zoe's face.

Unable to stop herself, she breathed it in. Her lungs froze first, then her tongue and the rest of her face. The paralysis travelled quickly down her neck, to her arms, but if it went further, she couldn't feel it. In an almost abstract, disjointed way, she wondered if she would shatter when she hit the floor, even as it rushed up at her. She fell facing one of the shopkeepers, whose glazed eyes stared at her, as though in a trance.

"It is the work of Boko Agwe's left hand, Madame Mama Zoe. His Iwa Voodoo spirits take you into waking death. It was not meant for you, but neither was that for which you came," the old woman lying beside her said. "Dey been watchin' you. Dey know all. Lady at the orphanage told dem you be comin'."

"We have to get her out, this pretty white girl."

"She made the Iwa spirits angry, sittin' in the wrong place, coming here to take the wrong thing. Madame Mama come here baby shoppin' no different like she buyin' a necklace with Erzulie on it. Come now."

"Maybe she just wanna be a mama like all the other women. How come you gotta hate her like that?"

"She can go buy white baby then."

Zoe could hear them, could see their shadows moving above her, but she couldn't move, couldn't scream. Had she broken her neck? Wasn't she supposed to be panicking? Why did her heart not speed up? It didn't even seem like she was breathing.

"You don' move, Madame Mama, until Boko tells you. Now he say lift your pretty white hand and stand up."

He leaned over her and, in her face, rattled a stick with three tiny skulls tied together at its end, wispy grass dangling from their jaws. She couldn't make out his features, his face backlit by the sunlight pouring through the hole in the ceiling of the shop. Zoe felt the spirit of another stir inside her body, lifting her hand into the air, the rest of her body following like a limp doll. As her own skin came into view, it looked a mottled grey. Her dust-dirtied blouse caught on the broken wood and stone around her as she was guided up and out of the shop, tearing into shreds.

"Hey, Boko. You collect enough white girls and maybe people can go zombie shoppin'."

The other man snorted. Was this the Boko the small girl at the cafe had cautioned her against offending? Had he really been watching her since her arrival?

"Who wants a skinny bitch? She look dead before the powder made her so."

Yes. Dead. I was pretty dead inside, but I didn't want this!

Zoe's body shuffled through the streets at the behest of the strange force inside her. She noticed absently how her left ankle bent the wrong way, was peripherally aware of bone stumps grinding against each other somewhere mid-shin, yet the spirit dictating her movements paid it no heed. All around her were people, dusty and weeping, or stumbling around aimlessly in shock, or crushed beneath broken, tumbled walls, or transfixed and immobile in burning vehicles. None of them took any notice of Zoe's strange condition, their own lives shattered or

136

ended. Her eyes rolled as she tried to get someone to help her. Voices drifted to her as she strained to find her own.

"We have to take him to the hospital!"

"There is no hospital! It's gone!"

"My father will die!"

"The army base! Get to the army base!"

Zoe tried to turn towards the evacuees, only to have the spirit occupying her snap her head back around with a sickening crunch, forcing her to continue forward. Hope sprung up from deep inside her when she saw her body headed toward a group of military personnel rushing about, carrying supplies, setting up tents, and trying to help the arriving injured.

Hope faded as she passed them. None so much as spared her a second glance. What was one lone, scruffy, confused person stumbling amongst the ruins of a city devastated by an earthquake? She hardly attracted notice. The essence inside her stopped her at the edge of a wide, shallow pit, looking like it had been hastily dug from a fresh gap in the earth. Broken corpses lined the bottom, neatly stacked out of the way. Her body turned around to face the man with the three skulls.

"I just din' want to carry you," he said and pushed her over into the pit.

The days Zoe lay in the pit came and went with her barely moving. More bodies were thrown over her until she could see only slivers of sunlight through their broken limbs. It must have been long past when she should have caught her flight back home, but she wasn't sure it mattered. Perhaps there was no longer any airport.

An old truck arrived. Over the course of an hour or so, Zoe and the others were dragged up and out of the pit and thrown onto the flatbed. She ended up facing another corpse whose dull eyes stared back at her. The dead man's eyelid fluttered. A tear rolled sideways across his face.

Her mind grew even more numb as the truck bounced along rubble-strewn streets, and her head banged against the wooden truck bed too many times to count. Eventually, the truck stopped, and judging by the sounds of the women screaming their family tombs were not to be further desecrated, they had arrived at a cemetery.

"What else can we do? There is already cholera breaking out! These must be buried."

Zoe was dragged off the truck and tossed into a small, unlit stone structure with several others. In the enclosed area, the smell of dust and rank death intensified. A trickle of sunlight slipped through a dirty, narrow window somewhere above her. This was one of the now-desecrated tombs, she feared. The muscles around her ribcage started to loosen, and she found she could finally blink one of her eyes. She huffed a few times, trying to get someone's attention, but couldn't get her voice to work. All she could do was watch as men with bricks and mortar closed off the opening of the tomb. The last thing she saw was a scabby rat run up to her face to lick and nibble at her eye she could not close.

"Erzulie Mansur speaks to you. I see her light surrounds your face." The voice was barely a gravelly whisper. She wasn't in here alone. Zoe gasped and her whole body convulsed as she fully awoke. Pins and needles burned like torturing, venomous ants as she again felt her heart thump painfully against her ribs, straining against the next forced intake of breath. At least she could move now, perhaps dig her way out, or yell until someone heard her. Her broken leg kicked against something as she floundered, and she screamed in agony.

"Erzulie says Madame Mama Zoe does not belong here, not with a little one inside her that Erzulie would protect. She is the guardian of all little children. Why is it only I can hear her, when she is speaking to you? You cannot hear the voices of the *loa*?"

"Wh-wha?"

"Erzulie says you already have baby. No need to have come here."

"Wh-o are—?"

"Another one Boko Agwe does not like. He throw us all in here."

"We...must...get...out... Help..."

Silence.

"Hello?" Zoe reached out, feeling only lanky bones and stickiness. She could see absolutely nothing. Angry and frustrated, still stiff and weak, Zoe screamed again, hearing only the answering chirp and scuffling of the rat, who had apparently returned with a group of friends.

"Erzulie," thought Zoe desperately, *"if you truly care about this child you say I'm carrying, please get me out!"*

"Erzulie has watched you a long time. Has heard Mama Zoe does not want to be alive. Has seen Mama Zoe comes here for a child and cannot see she has her own baby. Drinking wine, thinking only of herself, she cannot see what she already has. Erzulie will take good care of the baby after she takes it back from you. It will serve as Iwa."

Take it back?

"Orévwa, Zoe."

Au revoir? Goodbye?

"No!"

The rats began their feast.

Jennifer Rahn is the author of the dark fantasy novels *The Longevity Thesis* and *Wicked Initiations*. She also has short stories in Dragon Moon Press' *Podthology*, and Space Puppet Press' *Strange Worlds* anthology. Jennifer has degrees in Pharmacology and Medical Sciences, and currently works in academia and the biotech industry. To find out more about Jennifer, go to:

<u>longevitythesis.ca</u>

THE BETTER OF TWO EVILS
by Philip 'Norvaljoe' Carroll
Lake Nyos Limnic Eruption, 1986

The ground was uneven, yet familiar to the young boy as he picked his way down to the lake in the fading light of early evening. The wooden pole gripped loosely in his hand stood twice the height of his ten-year-old frame.

Joseph eyed the shoreline warily as his uncle's small herd of cattle crested the ridge and followed him down the broad bank. The lake water was smooth as glass, nestled in the crater of an extinct volcano. At an hour much later than he planned, long shadows stretched across the lake. It would be fully dark before the cattle were watered and heading back to their pen in Joseph's small village. He clicked and whistled his frustration at the slow moving beasts, though nothing he did had any effect on the animals.

Joseph shook his head and turned his attention back to the lake. He walked the last few steps to within a yard of the water's edge. Walking the length of the bank for some distance, all the while thrusting the pole into the shallow water and mud, he searched for crocodiles. He was surprised and only cautiously relieved to find none. Years had passed since at least one of the creatures weren't concealed in the shallow mud awaiting the opportunity to snatch one of the drinking cattle from the shore.

Before he could turn to call the meandering herd again, Joseph saw something floating a few yards out in the black water. The body of a small child bobbed face down in the gently undulating waves of the mountain lake. A chill crept up his spine.

Joseph had seen dead children before. The village was poor. Disease and malnourishment were common. Perhaps because the body was half-submerged in the water or because of the darkness, something looked odd about the child. The head was too big, or round, or out of proportion to the rest of its body, and Joseph stood frozen to the bank.

Something raked across the bare skin of his sweat covered back. He screamed in surprise and jumped forward. He lost his hold of his pole as he hit the slurry of mud beneath the shallow water of the bank. He danced a comical jig to regain his balance, losing the battle to stay upright and floundered frantically to get to his knees while searching blindly in the water for his pole. Panic pounded in his ears until the huffing, slobbering cow bent to drink from the lake where Joseph knelt.

"Damn cows," the boy cursed. He got to his feet and fished around until he found the pole on the bank.

During all the excitement the dead child had floated close enough to the shore for Joseph to reach it with his pole. He edged the body into the mud and rolled it onto its back.

The stench of rotten flesh overwhelmed him as the lifeless eyes glared from the water-swollen face. He fought against the urge to vomit and lost. He spewed what remained of his meager dinner across the bloated abdomen and emaciated arms of the child.

Only as Joseph turned away did enough starlight reveal the creature's unnatural maw. Its wide rictus smile split the face nearly from ear to ear. Fleshy, swollen lips pulled back to expose row upon row of wicked pointed, razor sharp teeth. A long serpent's tongue lolled out one side of its mouth like a separate creature.

"Demon," Joseph whispered and crossed himself.

The cow which had startled Joseph retreated to its companions in a nervous stomping and blowing clump halfway back up to the ridge of the ancient caldera. A narrow slice of waning moon sat just above the horizon and would soon follow the sun.

In the weak glow of the fading moon, Joseph saw another of the dead creatures bob to the surface. Dread boiled in the pit of his stomach and squeezed the air from his lungs. He gasped shallowly and fought blackness closing inside his head.

Another creature surfaced and joined the previous in its slow progress to the shore. Not dead. Neither were dead and were joined first by a few, then by many. As the vile, shambling, creatures lethargically stumbled up to the shore, they were a numberless, seething nightmare mass.

More demons pressed up to the shallow water at shore where they paused, shuddered, and shifted about as if finally coming awake. Red pinpoints of light flashed hate and evil from the heads of the shadows, back lit by the retreating moon. They shoved and jostled their companions to move as close to the shore as they could, but never left the water.

Joseph edged back from the assembling creatures until one of them looked his direction, and he felt his heart go cold. He tried to back further, afraid to look away from the mounting army of demons, but his feet rooted to the ground. The creatures hissed and chittered when they noticed the lone boy but held their place as if unable to set foot on the dry ground.

In the lake, well beyond the continually surfacing hoard, the water boiled and steamed, and glowed red.

The turbulence slowly increased, moving toward the shore. Waves sloshed against the mass of fidgeting and hissing demons congregating at the water's edge. As the boiling water grew in intensity so did the waves it gave off, until they crashed against the diminutive fiends. Some were tossed about by the current and dragged back into the lake while others climbed on the backs of their comrades and dug into them with razor claws.

A great glowing giant of a demon rose up through the bubbling turbulence and towered above its diminutive relatives. Its body cast intense red light as it climbed to its full height. The lake appeared on fire, alive with flickering waves, as the creature strode to the shore. Steaming water coursed off its glowing, scaled hide. Horns protruded from its temples and down the back of its neck. Brilliant ruby tusks jutted forward from the corners of its mouth.

In three long steps the monster reached the scrambling, struggling hoard at the shore. It screamed and swiped up five of the creatures in its massive hand and bit off their heads with its long reptilian jaws. Swallowing in one effortless gulp, it cast the limp bodies into the glowing water behind. It screamed again, ichor from the dead creatures running from the corners of its mouth and dripping from its tusks.

The glowing giant surveyed the shore, and its eyes fell on Joseph. It licked the residue of ichor from its lips and spat onto the shore beside the boy. The ground erupted in flames, smoldering and billowing thick oily smoke. The creature tipped its head back and emitted an articulated, barking scream into the crystal clear sky of the moonless night.

In a rush the creatures swarmed toward Joseph like the crashing waves on the shore.

Joseph watched in a trance, the ground burning at his side, the small black, creatures rushing toward him. The giant waited in the lake. The diminishing waves lapped at its ankles. Its scaled body was in the form of a man with a long tail like a lizard and the head of a horned snake. Its throat pulsed as it raised its open mouth to the sky and emitted a long, hissing scream.

Joseph's mind dulled further with each rapid shallow breath yet he felt the approaching hoard like an oncoming sneeze; weak, tickling, and inevitable. Even before they reached him, the demon's psychic hunger pulled at Joseph's soul. His every nerve was aflame, and his skin flayed itself from his body inside out. A soundless scream of agony locked in his paralyzed throat.

His body shuddered as the oily black creatures fell upon him and carried him to the ground. Their very touch burned like fire as they sucked his flesh with their swollen lips and licked him with their serpentine tongues. Each contact took with it a small piece of his agony-wracked soul until with a final crack, as of breaking bones, the last shreds of his living-self tore from his convulsing frame.

The demons rushed forward and fed on every life force they could find along the banks of the lake. The cattle, crocodiles, mice, and other small creatures fell prey to the insatiable fiends.

The rolling wave of hunger-crazed demons crested from the lake and ebbed away down the path of least resistance, along the bank of the lake, over the natural dam, and down the valley to the north. The glowing giant stepped onto dry ground. Its entire body shuddered with pleasure at the coming feast, and its face split into a long reptilian smile.

Philemon Mopani rolled over on the thin grass mat and tried to find a comfortable position for his twisted body. The gross curvature of his spine made it impossible to be comfortable on his back for any length of time. He stared drowsily into the darkness. A thatched roof hung above, though he couldn't truly see it. Something nagged at the back of his mind, and he couldn't place what, as if it were up there, hiding in the thatch. The more he struggled to place his unease the more awake he became, and thus, more agitated. Perhaps a quick trip to the outhouse would help.

Philemon struggled to his feet. His crippled body leaned to the right, shortened and bent by eighteen years of spastic reflexes. He wobbled to the door, carefully avoiding his snoring parents and brothers and sisters scattered about the dirt floor.

He was fast for his size. With long strides with his good leg and a quick bounces off the toes of the shorter, rigid right leg, he quickly made his way from the round mud-brick house to the outhouse in the middle of the circular village. Unable to speak many words, most thought him stupid, yet he could perfectly imitate the whistles and chirps of any bird he heard. He paused a moment at the metal door to the wooden outhouse and called to the several night birds in the trees close by.

Sitting was always more comfortable for the crippled boy than lying on the thin grass mat. He soon dozed off where he sat, his chin resting in the palm of one hand, the elbow on his knee.

Philemon's eyes snapped open. Something was wrong. He felt dread, like ants, crawling over his skin. Cold sweat formed small rivulets down his neck and spine. He listened intently for what had awoken him, but no such noise repeated. Then the cause hit him; there were no night bird sounds. The insects neither buzzed nor chirped, and the cattle, which always seemed to make noise throughout the night, were silent.

Philemon eased open the heavy metal door, which screeched like a peacock in the dead silence of the uncanny night. Nothing moved or seemed out of ordinary, if you discounted the silence. Perhaps there were lions, or hyena close by, yet he didn't believe it himself.

He dashed for the security of his home, leaping and springing like a gazelle, when the flood of demons overtook the village.

The wave of creatures crashed into the village, spilled around and through the brick huts like glistening, liquid ebony. Demons coalesced around the huts and fell on the inhabitants, sucking and licking the souls from their resistant bodies. Others of the fiends clung to the huts, pawed at the thatched roofs, and slavered on the mud bricks.

The creatures flowed past and around Philemon, and like a sudden mudslide, picked him up and carried him along. The creatures foamed and slobbered and smacked their rubbery lips as they dashed about in search of souls from which they could feed. Small groups stayed around each of the homes, but the majority of the fiends, no larger than Philemon, continued further down the valley.

Philemon leapt along with the fiends, their leathery skin slick with oily sweat, pungent like stagnant water. The boy quickly began to fatigue and knew he couldn't maintain the demon's pace much longer. He would either fall and be trampled by the creatures or be recognized as a foreigner in their midst and fall prey to their insatiable appetite.

147

Salvation came in the form of a tree. The creatures' combined momentum carried him directly beneath a low hanging branch, which he grabbed with his good hand and swung up to cling with his knees. As soon as he had his breath back, he shimmied up higher and out of sight into the branches above.

Refreshed and invigorated by their recent feeding, the demons pressed together at the bottom of the long valley. They hooted, hissed, and screamed, and bobbed rhythmically as a unified, throbbing mass of ichor.

Philemon felt a short rhythmic vibration in the branches where he clung. Each beat increased in intensity until a booming sound resonated above the chatter and screams of the massed fiends. The jumping and writhing creatures below and the branches of the tree where he clung glowed faintly red with reflected light. Philemon reasoned the village must have caught fire, but turning in that direction, the boy nearly fell from his perch as terror turned his insides to water. A giant demon approached with long booming strides soon bringing it directly under the quaking boy.

He had to do something or the giant would see him perched in the branches. He could drop back down into the crowd and conceal himself among the creatures, or even try to make his way through them to safety.

As he prepared to drop back to the earth, he crossed himself as the priests had taught him, which gave him an idea. The priests were always praying and had spent much of their time teaching the children prayers. Philemon wished he could remember an appropriate prayer for such a predicament, but the priests had considered him stupid and gave up on teaching him after a short time. In the depths of his fear, he could only remember one prayer and could only form a few of the actual words.

"Ouwa Fahddah," he said and looked down to see if any of the demons had heard. They were much too busy cheering their leader's arrival.

"Heabben...hollow name....." Tears sprang to the boys eyes, and he cursed his disability. How could God hear and answer such a poorly uttered prayer?

"Gib, day, bread.....Porgib......lead not...." and he remembered the part he wanted.

"Delibber, prom, Ebil," he shouted and looked up into the night sky.

The stars were faint pin pricks, through the billowing dust. A blinding white light and a clap of thunder shook the demons from their feet and nearly dropped Philemon from his hiding place. Space and time broke open. Rushing winds ruffled silver, razor-edged feathers on the great eagle-wings of twelve massive creatures emerging through a rent to stand side by side. Their glowing white bodies were silhouetted to black by the brilliance of the dimensional opening.

The demons jumped up and down and screamed and hooted. They tore at one another with their filthy, pointed teeth and raked razor claws across the arms and backs of their fellows. They shrieked and howled in anticipation of the coming fight with glee. They chattered and barked their incomprehensible demon language at the newly arrived enemy.

Philemon clung to the branches of the tree as the new creatures beat their wings. The gale threatened to tear him from the branch and carried dust into the air, spinning it in small tornados, lifting demons from their feet and casting the screaming creatures yards away.

The twelve stood three times the height of the hissing, spitting, demons. Short white fur bristled over rippling muscles of the creatures' chests and shoulders. They flared their wide nostrils, snarled, and bared long baboon-like muzzles with wicked, oversized canines and pearl-black teeth.

They formed a line across the narrow valley, their wing tips barely touching, and screamed at the hell spawn, scrambling to recover from the gale.

Each of the twelve gripped a flaming white sword in one clawed hand. The skin of their faces, hands, and feet, radiated light, a pale reflection of the intense light from the portal at their backs.

The innumerable, demonic hoard laughed, hooted, and cavorted about at the feet of the patiently waiting twelve.

Wind burst anew from the dimensional gap as it enlarged to permit three more creatures to enter the mortal realm. The demons screamed as if hell itself had come to reclaim them. The enraged fiends hissed and spat at the newcomers. Unlike their previous brethren, the bodies of the three were hairless, and they wore a loose white girdle wrapped around their loins. They stood chest, shoulders, and head above the twelve and had only a single eye in the middle of their brows. Each carried a silver longbow, strung with gold and nocked with arrows of lightning. Translucent leathery bat-wings unfurled behind the newcomers as they glided forward and took positions behind the first twelve.

With each passing moment the demons worked themselves into a greater frenzy, shifting back and forth, hooting and screeching, but never advancing beyond an unseen border as if a single step would break the dam and begin a flood of soulless fiends.

A single personage stepped through, moved forward, and stood behind the left shoulder of the centermost of the three. Head and shoulders above the three, gossamer silk shrouded the One's body. Colors shifted and swirled across the silk in random patterns of more hues than are known to the earthly sphere. Hair of pure white fell to the shoulders. Where the eyes should have been were only shallow depressions of unbroken skin, yet when Philemon looked upon him, he felt exposed, measured, and judged.

Light dimmed as the dimensional rift re-sealed. The demon hoard was suddenly silent and unmoving.

Like a loose sail catching a sudden wind the last one unfurled silken butterfly wings. Its body burned with white-hot light and shown like the sun at midday. Wings beat slowly back and forth, dividing and reflecting the entire spectrum of visible light in a glorious, kaleidoscope of shifting, confusing color.

Are these few creatures sent from God to fight the demons and their giant lord? Are these angels?

The demons went mad, screaming, and clawing at their eyes in their sudden blindness. Their fury whipped up to a fevered pitch. They bared rows of vicious, sharp rotted teeth, hissed with fetid breath, and screamed as they tore at one another with filthy, disease-ridden claws. Smoking ichor dripped from long, raw, gashes in the demon's glistening black bodies. The acid blood burned the grass and earth wherever it fell.

While the demons went mad at the sight of the radiant, multi-hued wings, Philemon only felt peace, comfort, and hope. Hope. *They must be angels.*

The demons fairly danced in anticipation and barely controlled hunger. They hopped from foot to foot, climbed atop one another and fought each other to move to the front of the teeming hoard. Like ocean foam piles on a beach, ceaselessly driven by storm winds, the slavering snarling demons piled higher and higher before the twelve.

The twelve baboon angels at the front, raised their flaming swords and bared their own teeth in snarls and growls, welcoming the infernal menace to meet the edge of their blades. To an unheard command, in unison, they placed their feet shoulder width apart and crouched, ready for battle.

The twelve didn't wait long. The demon lord raised its scaled arms, clawed at the night sky with radiant, ruby-taloned, fingers, and screamed at the top of its lungs, a high-pitched ululation. The call faded, and the demon hoard screamed and launched toward their waiting enemy.

The insignificant creatures threw themselves directly at their opposition's front line. With broad swipes, the muscular sword wielding angels, severed fiends of their arms, heads, and torsos. Black, smoking ichor spurted from dying bodies and soaked into the ground as the demons' fetid bodies piled at the clawed feet of the angels. The coarse, white, hair of the angels' legs quickly stained indiscernible from the lifeless forms around them. With their free hands the angels snatched the occasional demon making it past their flaming swords and tore out the creature's throats with their canine jaws.

The demons drew back as it became obvious they couldn't penetrate the angel line straight on. They broke into two screaming, slavering groups and rushed at both ends of the line, to gain ground behind the twelve.

With a few deft steps the twelve formed a circle with their backs to the three and the One; their massive eagle's wing's overlapped to form an impenetrable wall.

The three angels within the circle of their smaller brethren formed a triangle and faced out toward the demons. Spinning, shimmering, arrows of lightning flew from the three archers' bows. They crackled and boomed with thunder, passing through the demon hoard. The white hot pulses of electricity cut down the creatures in long, broad swaths.

The One sightless challenger towered above its brethren, it's broad, butterfly wings unfurled, casting the battle in brilliant, shifting, light. It never moved; it's face toward the demon lord.

As the divided hoard of fiends met at the far side of the ring, they clashed with one another and blindly gnashed on their comrades with razor teeth set in festering black gums. They clawed at each other's throats until their lord waded forward, through the tide of shining black bodies.

The flaming-red, creature bellowed in rage, and moved close to the tree where Philemon hid. When it screamed, Philemon made to cover his ears, lost his balance, and fell from the tree. The boy lay still among the feet of the screaming, dancing demons. Hoping their lord hadn't seen his fall, he peered through those milling around him. The demon lord looked his direction.

The red giant leapt with unexpected agility to within a meter of Philemon's feet. It snatched up an unsuspecting fiend and cast it over the angels and into the midst of the struggling, contending demons. The demon lord stood silent. Its glowing, soulless, eyes cut across the scene of mayhem and confusion, and it bellowed again, a long, slowly ululating wail. The hoard stopped and turned toward their master.

Philemon felt, as much as saw, wave upon wave of additional demons as they flowed endlessly down the valley from the lake and joined the minions crowding the angels' defensive ring. The demon lord barked and coughed out unintelligible syllables of its articulated language. Demons screamed in glee and rushed to their lord hooting and jumping at their master with hands outstretched. The glowing giant laughed, scooped an armful of the small creatures and cast them over the heads, wings, and swords of the twelve outer angels. The broad baboon creatures wrinkled their muzzles and bared their teeth as the creatures flew ungracefully over their heads.

Within the ring the three retreated to the center and overlapped their leathery bat wings. The myriad colors of the One shown clearly through the translucent skin, but faded as the One wrapped itself in its own wings, and its light dimmed.

As the flock of hurled demons sailed toward the angel of the three most directly facing them, the angel let a bolt of lightning fly from its longbow, instantly vaporizing the airborne foe.

A single demon who survived fell at the feet of the three, crawled to its feet, and thrust its razor talons into the soft flesh of the closest batwing. The angel grunted in pain as the demon's claw cut though its tender skin, but never lost eye contact with the demon lord ten yards away. It wrapped the tearing, clawing demon in its bleeding wing and casually tossed the fiend onto the back of one of the twelve. The silver razor edged feathers of the majestic eagle wings shredded the creature to lifeless slices of demon flesh before it reached the ground.

The demon lord screamed again and scooped up a second volley of screaming, struggling fiends to cast at the center of the angelic host. Amid the screaming

154

biting fiends was Philemon, the air pressed from his lungs by the demon lord's strangling grip.

He flew through the air toward the one-eyed angel, its bow drawn, and its crackling lightning bolt aimed between Philemon's eyes. At the very moment the boy expected the angel to loose the arrow and obliterate him and his screaming, struggling companions, the angel fired the bolt harmlessly into the ground behind the nearest baboon angel and dropped the silver long bow. It spread its bat wings out wide and deftly plucked Philemon from the air with its empty hands. The demons sailed past to be batted to the ground by the strong leathery wings.

Philemon knew nothing more of the world around him. His mind felt as one with the angel who cradled him in his arms. They were angels. He knew without doubt. Not the kind of angel who sings *Hallelujah* or *brings tidings of great joy*. These were the angels sent to protect mankind from the fiend of the infernal pit, the angels who were sent to combat demons who escape from hell.

Philemon felt the angel's emotions and was surprised. He expected hate and anger toward the demons. Instead the boy perceived pained pity and regret, as a man would feel for a brother, whom, having made bad choices, must now be punished.

Philemon also felt the angel's sorrow for the villagers who suffered at the hands of the demons. He felt the circle of angels around him who fought with their foe for righteous retribution.

When Philemon came to himself, he lay at the feet of the One, within the circle of the three who rotated in a clockwise motion as they fired bolt after bolt, crackling and burning through the mass of demons.

Philemon knelt at the feet of the one angel, peered through the angel's semi-transparent wings and watched the battle progress. Filtered through the translucent skin of the angel's bat wing, the brilliant ruby glare was gone from the demon lord's eyes, and only its eternal malice and hatred shown through.

The mounting hoard of demons swelled with continuous reinforcements from the lake. They threw themselves anew upon the swords of the twelve like a tidal wave throws itself on the rocky beach. The creatures were dashed to pieces by the angels' swords. The angels snarled and hacked at the endless sea of shiny black bodies.

A song, a single voice, rose above the clamor of grunts, gasps, and screams. The One sang with a voice like pure crystal bells and wind through mountain trees. The demons shuddered and faltered momentarily while the angels took courage and redoubled their assault. Those in the outer ring hacked, grabbed, and tore while the inner three fired searing bolts of electricity.

As the angels fought they moved. The twelve rotated their ring, slowly in a counter clockwise direction. Slower yet, imperceptibly slow compared to the rabid creatures who fought them, the twelve moved their ring of fiery swords, ichor stained teeth, and razor edged wings, inch by inch closer to the demon lord. Inside the ring, the three angels rotated in a clockwise direction at a faster pace to allow each a turn at shooting flying demons from the air and dealing with the unfortunate few to land within the circle, still alive.

The One, sightless, swaddled in its own gossamer wings, sang on, as if oblivious to the horrific battle which waged around it.

The demon lord never tired of hurling arm load after arm load of its minions to their soulless death, though the hapless creatures grew wary of their lord and did their best to stay out of its reach. Consequently the angel ring met little resistance as it moved itself within a few feet of the towering, crimson giant.

Without warning the angels of the outer ring, nearest the demon lord, faltered. They stumbled, and the defensive circle broke open. A hooting, screaming mob of the grotesque creatures flowed into the circle and charged toward the One, still singing and protected by the three. The demon lord screamed and barked a long, segmented laugh. Leaping and dancing, it followed its jubilant minions into the circle.

The glowing, smoldering demon barely passed within the boundaries of the angel circle, when those who had fallen jumped back to their feet and re-closed the ring. Once in position, all twelve of the outer ring turned to face into the circle, their razor armored wings interlocked, an effective barrier against those demons left outside the ring.

In a few swift blows from the twelve, the lesser creatures were eliminated. The three fired bolt after bolt of lightning into the crimson creature's chest, forcing it to stumble back into the flaming swords of the twelve. With each strike their swords burned brighter as the demon lord's inner flame dimmed until all that shone was the giant creatures glowing eyes and ruby tusks. The demon lord threw itself from side to side, weakly, as if searching for an escape, but lacking the strength to press its way through. With a final impotent roar and an elongated hiss, the demon lord fell to the ground, its inner glow eternally extinguished.

The demon hoard fell still and silent, staring in the direction of their fallen leader.

The angels didn't wait. They broke their circle and fell upon the small creatures. They slashed with their swords of fire and tore with their ichor stained teeth. The stunned demons screamed and fled back up the valley.

The One unfurled its wings, picked Philemon gently from the ground, cradled him in the crook of its arm, and sent brilliant streaming light up the valley after the fleeing foe, the twelve hot on their heels. They cut the vile creatures down as they ran. The demons' flight was impeded at first by reinforcements flowing down from the lake, but the newcomers soon understood the depth and breadth of the rout and quickly retreated with the battle-wizened comrades.

The three angels, followed by the One made their way slowly toward the lake. The three vaporized the carcasses of the fallen demons with searing bolts of power from their singular eyes. The One purged the ichor soaked soil with its flickering, shifting, kaleidoscope of colored light and the gentle beating of its wings.

At the lake, the fleeing demons hit the water en masse and dove for the passage back to the infernal pits of hell. Unlike their arrival into the human world, slow, systematic, and calm, they frantically fought one another to gain access to the tunnels which would lead them home.

Carbon dioxide trapped in the volcanic sediment began an avalanche in reverse. First small amounts of the gas bubbled toward the surface of the lake. The heavy silt, dislodged by the smaller bubbles made way for more, until with a rush, thousands of cubic kilograms of the suffocating gas burst from the lake. The heavy cloud swelled hundreds of feet into the air and slowly rolled over the edge of the ancient crater and down the valley to the north.

The angels stood on the lip of the natural dam and looked sadly down the valley. Philemon slept peacefully in the arms of the One, wrapped tightly in the silken angel wings. All evidence of the demons scoured from the earth. The bodies of thousands lay dead in their homes and villages. People, cattle, creatures great and small, dead, as if killed by the cloud of gas.

The One returned Philemon to his family's home and placed his bent form on the only unoccupied mat among his dead family members. The eyeless face looked down on the sleeping, crippled boy as it spread its butterfly wings as wide as it could in the cramped hut. The whitewash walls of Philemon's home were bathed in the infinite hues of the angel's light. The One reached out with a finger and traced the boy's curved spine, across his hip, and down the stiff right leg. Philemon's body relaxed and became whole.

The angel looked around the room at the boy's family. Father, mother, brothers and sisters, all dead. A terrible life for the boy to return to even whole. The angel touched each of the lifeless forms on the forehead and chest, returning their souls to their bodies.

Outside the round mud brick home, a clap of thunder shook the ground and the air around. A rift opened between the mortal realm and that of the angels. Sixteen guardians returned to heaven to await their next mission.

Philip 'Norvaljoe' Carroll is a husband, father and grandfather, an army trained Certified Orthotist and dreamer. While he physically lives in the Central Valley of California, his mind is typically in other places. He has been writing for about four years and has had short stories printed in several benefit anthologies. His novel *The Price of Friendship* can be found at Podiobooks.com. He is an editor at Flying Island Press. To find out more about Philip, go to:

www.thepriceoffriendship.blogspot.com

IN MEMORIES OF DUST
By Chris Ringler
Dust Storms of Nebraska, 1934

God, how I hated this place. This land of ignorance and graveyards. This place with no memory. A land with no memory is a land with no soul and such is this place, this America, this Nebraska.

I miss my green isle, the smell of the ocean, and the feel of the grass beneath my feet. This is a land with many ghosts. Too many ghosts.

My Declan was just another among them, another voice echoing in the winds as they blew across the plains. I could hear him in my dreams, calling out to me from the darkness, calling out to me as he died.

My darkness came to me as a girl and took my sight, the curse that kept me from him at the end. He called for me from the great pond out back where we used to take supper in the early days. Called for me, screaming for me until he was gone. Now I was alone in a strange country with too many gods and drowning in sand.

With Declan's passing, I preferred being by myself to having someone come here to work the land. Preferred it to the thought of marrying a man out of frailty and need. No one would till that soil, not so long as I lived, and even if the end was coming it was not yet here. Not yet.

I kept the garden; the only thing I could tend without sight, and kept it green. The rest could rot for all I cared. Oh, I got by, I survived, but I was a broken old woman with a stone lying atop her heart, and little was all I needed. Was all I wanted. And that was what I got, little and none, until the storms. Until the sand. Until the thing that came with both.

The storms began a year and a half after Declan died. The air turned cool, and the dust came and blotted out the sun for hours at a time. The ground was dead, the preacher told me the last day he made it out. The ground was dead and nothing would grow because of the dust that blew. The bitter irony of it all is even had Declan lived, we would have lost our dream. The ground had been burned by the sun and the seeds wouldn't hold any longer. The preacher marveled I had been able to keep my meager garden alive, but I had the well right there, and the protection of a giant tree, and maybe the fates and fairies looked after me.

Nothing could survive the dust though and eventually even the garden died, buried by the dirt that filled the air every day. With the dust came the cold and the darkness and ruin. I heard stories from the preacher that people in town were leaving, running south and north and east and west, anywhere they could to get away from the darkness. There had been murders, suicides, and so much sadness, all attributed to the Lord's wrath, a plague of dust.

For me the darkness was a comfort. I had been blind so long the light meant nothing to me, the sun was little solace, and for me there was nothing to see but heartache so to not have to feel the warmth of the sun on me was almost a comfort. Almost. I'd taken to walking to Declan's grave every day at supper time to talk with him, but the dust was getting so bad I knew I couldn't make the trip anymore. I had almost gotten lost twice. If I did, what then? One more, one more trip, I promised him and no more until the dust left or I joined him.

The storms came more and more frequently and much of the town was gone. Every day was filled with a blizzard of dust and it seemed to have wiped everyone away. Even the preacher was gone. He had brought me supplies and had sat down to lunch with me but told me he wouldn't be back. This place was dead. The land, the sky, all of it dead, the victim of God's Justice.

He asked me to leave with him with all I could take. I refused, resigned to die with my Declan if that was God's Will, or to find what path might lie ahead in the dust if that be His Will. Either way, I had chosen to stay.

That night the storm howled and rocked the house, and I decided I would move to the cyclone cellar and see out the worst of it. If the Lord took me, so be it. Until such time I would stay and defend my land from the dust.

I had been sweeping the house daily, feeling the dirt with my bare feet so I could sweep it, and wiping down the cupboards and furniture but it was a battle I had lost.

The storms were too bad now. The wind screamed and thrashed through the night. I heard the great crash of something near the house and hid myself under the covers. When I woke and made my way out of the bedroom I found the front door open and an inch of dirt on the floor. I found the same in the kitchen and more dust on the countertops. I thought I was in a nightmare. This wasn't my home any longer, this was a tomb. My life, what was left of it, was being buried. I fell to my knees and cried, cried for an hour at how we had lost everything here in this damned place. Cried about how much suffering one could take before they broke for good.

After I was all cried out, I knelt there on the floor and thought about my Declan and what he had sacrificed to give me this dream. I had enough of mourning. I got up, brushed myself off and dressed.

The preacher had put the food he had brought with him into the cellar so it would be safe. All I needed was water. Declan had put beds and linens down there. I could fasten blankets to the door to keep out the dust. The house wasn't safe anymore. I was going to wait it out, wait it out as long as I could in the cellar. When it passed, I would take to the road and find God's path for me, wherever it led to.

When I was dressed, I went out to say goodbye to my love. I was out halfway to the pond and his grave when the storm returned with such force I fell beneath its blow and crawled until I found a tree to hang on to. The winds cut across the land and howled as the dust slashed at my face. I felt tears mix with blood, and I prayed. I prayed to God to save me, to save me and return me to the safety of my home.

As I cowered behind the tree, the ground shook with a great roar from where my Declan lay, and I clutched the trunk of the tree tighter. I cocked my ear to listen and heard it again, a roar and a great splash of water and the ground shook as if from an earthquake. I didn't know what I was hearing, but I didn't care to find out. I got up and ran wildly toward where I thought my home was but tripped over something in a matter of steps.

Lying there, I felt a wave of ice cold air on me and heard something like heavy breath. I lifted my head, felt eyes on me, and the presence of something big. A scream welled in my throat, but I refused it. I was near the pond and could smell the water on this thing, could feel the cold it radiated, and heard it struggling for air. I began to crawl slowly, hoping the storm had confused it and it wouldn't follow me, allowing me to get away. I had made it far enough away I couldn't smell it and started to stand. It roared again, and the earth shook beneath me.

It came for me.

The fear I had held at bay overtook me. I screamed, and my mouth filled with dust. I ran choking from it, praying I wouldn't fall. The beast howled, sounding pained, and I imagined how scared it must be, how horrifying this world must be if its life was spent in the great pond where my Declan had drowned.

I ran. My chest burned as I struggled to suck in more air and push myself forward. Another roar and fire erupted along my back. I was sent flying forward into the ground. Blood poured from my back, and I stung from the dust blowing into the open wound.

Dizzy from pain, I heard the beast come forward. I was prone to it, my body weak, and the world became faint and distant. I dug my hands into the ground looking for purchase and felt the cold of it as it bent forward to sniff at me. It growled and pushed at me with something like a finger and roared again. And why, why was this happening? Why did this thing pursue me? Was its rage at the world, or me, or God? Was I just the first thing it had seen when it came out of its home to see why the world was consumed by the dust? I dug my hands into the dirt and there, oh God *there*, I felt something cold and wooden and wrapped my hand around it. My hoe. I had found my hoe. I was in my garden. The beast had thrown me into my garden.

The world seemed frozen as the dust tapered off. I felt the sudden warmth of the sun on me and that must have distracted the beast as it had forgotten me for the moment. I got a firm grip on the hoe and rolled onto my back. I heard the thing grunt, its attention back on me, and it wrapped a hand around me, its hand half my size and powerful. The dust had stopped, and as the beast tried to pick me up, I screamed and pulled the hoe from the dirt and swung it at the thing. I felt the hoe strike and was dropped immediately to the ground as it howled in pain and rage. I pulled the hoe free, got to my feet, and began swinging wild.

Miss.

Miss.

Miss.

Strike.

The thing howled again, and my body erupted in fire as it struck out and knocked me onto the back porch. I had lost the hoe and crawled as quickly as I could. It roared, after me again. I had made it inside the house, crawling across the dirt and wincing with every movement, hoping I was safe. I heard it at the porch, too big to follow me inside, the squealing of wood being torn apart warned me as it came after me.

All was still for a moment before the storm returned in force. The thing screamed as the storm swallowed the beast, and my heart ached for all I heard was utter and absolute fear as the sands came back. It roared and turned its fear and rage toward the house, and the porch collapsed into the dirt. The thing threw itself at the door again, and again, and again, trying to get to me. Desperate to destroy me even if it meant it died in the process. As it came at me, I crawled forward and prayed I would find a way to fight back. I heard the door splinter, and the thing slammed its body into it, its rage turned to madness. I stood up and fell against the counters and grabbed anything I could get my hands on to turn and throw at the beast.

Pan.

Spoon.

Egg.

My hand closed on a bag of something. I spun around and threw it at the thing with all I had left as it shattered the door's frame and entered the kitchen. I heard the bag explode against the thing and turned to find something else but had reached the corner of the room. Nothing was left.

I turned, faced the beast and held my hands out, determined to fight it until it took me. For a full minute nothing happened. The only sound was the wind driven dirt and dust that hit the side of the house. Stuck in the doorway, the thing blocked much of the dust, but its silence scared me more than anything. I could smell the thing, smell the pond on it, smell the sweat on it, and could smell something else. Something I couldn't quite place. The silence was finally broken by a low mewling sound that grew louder and louder, sounding like sobs.

I smelled something new in the air, something hot, like fire, like fire and salt, and then jumped at a loud crash as the beast fell. I heard it wheezing and took a step forward. The thing growled, but the growl quickly faded, replaced by the mewling and a low moan. Another step and another moan. It thrashed on the floor. I heard a crash like furniture hitting the wall. The beast growled again then was silent a moment and in the silence I heard something sizzling and popping.

It was dying.

I moved carefully forward. It growled again though more a moan now. It tried to move away from me, I heard it thrash against the kitchen table, but it was stuck in the doorway so it stilled and simply breathed shallowly. I approached it until my foot kicked it. The thing whimpered. I carefully knelt and the smell of burning filled my head, the scent of the water long gone.

The bag must have been salt, it had to have been, and this thing was dying from it. Burning because of it. Outside the dust storm retreated, and the thing before me breathed less and less. I laid a hand against it, and its skin was thick and scaly. It reminded me of a snake until I felt where it was breathing from and wondered what beautiful, horrible thing it was that was dying before me, and what God had birthed it.

I ran my hand over it until I felt its smooth head. It whimpered beneath my touch. I petted it and it shuddered. I felt its heavy hand fall against my lap and it whined pitifully. I felt my dress soaked, probably from blood. The beast panted as I petted, rolled toward me, and was still. It was gone, and I was left alone with its body. I was crying but uncertain why. Uncertain if I cried of the thing or myself, or for both of us and the damnable fate that had brought us together this way.

I knelt beside the thing for a long while, breaking into sobs for it, for me, for Declan, and for dreams denied. Whatever this thing was, it had been as frightened of me as I was of it, and in the end it had died a useless death. The land was dead, the sky was dead, but the preacher didn't realize that in this place, even the water was dead. I wondered if the beast had family and a last sob escaped me before I forced myself up and away from it. It was time to move on.

I had believed in that green, green dream, and in my husband with all my heart, but the dream had died, just as Declan had. I wasn't dead. I lived, and I had to move on. I would find a new dream, and I would cling to it until my last days were upon me, knowing this place had not beaten me, not in the end.

I carefully made my way over the thing and through the wreckage of the porch. My back screamed with pain. I wasn't sure where I would go but started walking carefully toward town, or where I thought town was, and turned my back on the past. I was alive, and I was determined to stay that way.

A long while later I heard something from back by the house, a long, mournful cry, and it brought more tears to my eyes. I wondered what had made it, and if it would choose to live as I had or to remain by the side of its partner and join with the land.

In the quiet parts of the night I can still hear its cry as if its memory were scratched not just on my mind but on the wind or the very land itself, forever scarring and branding it with its mark. Forever part of the dust.

Chris Ringler was raised in Linden, Michigan, where he lived and attended school. He fell in love with writing as a teenager when he started writing short stories and began working on fanzines with friends. In 1999 *Back From Nothing*, a short story collection was published by University Editions. Since that time, Chris has finished writing a novel, a children's series and has been published in *Bare Bone* and *Cthulhu Sex Magazine*. He has also received Honorable Mention in *The Year's Best Fantasy and Horror* twice. Chris is a writer, artist, weirdo, and creator of the Flint Horror Convention. To find out more about Chris, go to:

grimringler.wordpress.com.

THE BEIJING MASKERADE
by Michael McGee
True Account of the SARS Epidemic, 2003

Back in 2003, about a month prior to me leaving the U.S. for my first trip to China, a friend told me I might want to delay my trip a bit because he'd heard a particularly virulent disease had broken out there. At that time, it had no name as I remember, but we'd soon come to know it as SARS.

Initially, I had planned to make my overseas trip a two-legged journey, spending the first ten weeks in China, and then on my way back, another three or four weeks in Japan. But hearing about the quarantining going on, where various governments had decided planes carrying passengers from China and Hong Kong might be isolated for ten days upon arrival, I thought this might be a pretty poor way to meet my Japanese friends—by spreading some lethal disease through their neighborhood.

So, a week before I was to leave I switched my flight arrangements. This would allow me to spend a month in Japan *first*, before moving on to China. Though this sounded like a good idea at the time, it would have rather interesting consequences. Because after spending some time with my friends both in Kyoto and Tokyo, I landed in Beijing on April 20 of that year, the very day the Mayor of Beijing made his fateful announcement that the city had not been particularly forthcoming about how bad SARS had become there. Of course, we would find out later the government had actually been hiding hospital patients outside the city, so officials could more, uhm, "accurately" log the reported number of SARS cases in Beijing—part of their attempt to head off an economic downturn in the capitol.

As a result, April 20 became the day when the panic in the city began to build into a quick crawl. Within a week, most of the 14 million people in Beijing were invisible, fearful of what was looking like the next great pandemic. Soon, the only groups of humans evident on the street were those lined up to purchase masks and disinfectant. An area called Wangfujing, one of the busiest shopping centers on Earth, replete with high-class malls and a gaggle of top-flight restaurants, and where people typically walked shoulder to shoulder amidst the human crush, overnight became a ghost town.

Beijing's subway, reeking of boiled vinegar, also emptied, except for a handful of courageous, or perhaps we'll call them "reckless", souls. Theaters were shut, museums closed down—in fact, any place where more than 25 people could possibly gather had their doors locked. To my great distress, this included Beijing's Internet cafés, which were the very portals I required to send my work back and forth to the States and thus keep myself gainfully employed as a book editor and writer. Without them, I knew I'd lose *further* editing contracts, and perhaps cripple my livelihood altogether.

For you see, my difficulties due to SARS were going to be a bit hard to explain since I had not bothered to tell some of the companies I edited books for that I was actually living abroad while doing my work—let alone living in China, suddenly the world's most unhealthy hotspot. And the reason I *hadn't* told them was because, as ubiquitous as Internet connections were around the world, many employers—fearing that some vague and shifting book deadline might be missed—were prone to panic, not so unlike the citizens of Beijing. Though admittedly it's not every day your average book editor, like me, walks into a global pandemic that mucks up the works. I figured the less my publisher employers knew, the better for all involved. No need for them to worry needlessly; I'd let them know if there was a *real* problem—you know, besides me possibly dying.

I, of course, knew the Internet was still there in China, I just wasn't sure exactly how to access it. And with things continuing to fold around me like that time-honored house of cards, what few remaining options I had were quickly disappearing.

Despite all this, I still wanted to make the most of my stay in Beijing. It was my first visit after all, and I had spent a pretty penny to get there—and stay there. I had even been far-sighted enough to pack some surgical masks before leaving California. *However*—and some folks will slap me here—*I never bothered to fish them out while I was in China.* The reasons for this I'll try to explain later, and you can draw your own conclusions. Instead, as few people as there were on the streets then, I was typically one of the sole holdouts traipsing about without a mask on. I was chastised repeatedly for this by my Beijing friends, but as I said, I'll try to explain the logic behind my actions later.

Early on in my stay in Beijing, I'd come across a rather neurotic New Yorker, a fellow whom I'll call Biff here, mostly because I can't remember his name offhand. He was in his late fifties and had a stringy Ben Franklin–like coiffure, with a beard and mustache combo underneath that was forever collecting daily deposits of food from his meals, like he was hoarding the stuff. At least I can't remember him ever combing out the edible bits, an act that would have been tantamount to Christmas for the local mice, I suppose. Every time we met to talk, before he ever put fork to mouth, I'd spot morsels from his lunch, say, last week Tuesday, nestled in the gray and tan shanks that descended to his shirt.

I suppose the most defining characteristic about Biff though was his paranoia. He'd left the United States fearing persecution by various government agencies who were supposedly out to, uhm, *get him*— for reasons that were always a bit fuzzy to me. And given Biff, who wasn't exactly your Jason Bourne type, I couldn't see our government really taking the time to bother with him, unless it was for something like smuggling contraband into the country under his chin. Nonetheless, he had a binder of news clippings he sometimes carried with him which he would occasionally unearth to back up his assertions. Pointing to this or that scientist's picture, as depicted in *The New York Times* or *Washington Post*, he outline some vague connection between them and the mysterious personal work he was involved in.

Don't get me wrong. It wasn't like Biff was really crazy or anything like that. He was a very intelligent fellow and quite savvy in many respects. It's just I don't think he'd thought through some things terribly well. For instance, if *I* had been trying to evade *Big Brother*, my first choice of relocation would not exactly have been China. But then, if I'd been Biff, I'd have actually brushed out my beard after every meal… Either way, Biff was a worried man—and a worried man at the epicenter of the SARS pandemic, no less.

In his concern about SARS, however, Biff was not alone—not by any means. And with that in mind, let me touch a little on some of the craziness that had taken hold in China at that time; a craziness human beings everywhere are prone to exhibit when facing the unknown... particularly an unknown that is *lethal*. For instance, despite people wearing masks everywhere, and even sometimes kissing with them on—there was a very famous and terribly cute photo of a young couple kissing in China this way—there were many people who actually took up *smoking* in order to combat SARS, pulling down their masks just long enough to take a puff from a cigarette. Some people thought the nicotine actually killed the SARS virus, or made it more difficult for you to contract the disease. Others believed smoking would shorten the length of the infection. Rumor had it that the WHO—the World Health Organization—had even *made* such an announcement on their web site, encouraging people to light up. Something which was not true.

A few people even touted the knock-out combo of cigarettes and hard liquor as a bona fide way of fighting the disease. This latter belief stemmed from the idea that with so many poisons fighting for the host body's best cells, they would cancel each other out.

Nevertheless, many people in China looked for hope in somewhat irrational remedies.

For instance, some thought that burning incense—and lots of it—would ward off SARS. Why? Because monasteries continually use incense, and the locals believed the monks never got sick.

Farmers in Guangdong province in southern China had deemed vinegar the best SARS-fighter. They would dump bottles of the stuff in their cooking, drink it straight, or with a little water. They would even pour a cupful of it and set the cup in the corner of a room as a SARS deterrent. Most of this vinegar application arises from an earlier belief, that boiling vinegar and letting its steam fill a room is a time-honored way of combating colds in China. The process was just taken a step further, the end result causing a run on vinegar in some parts of their country.

Some people instead devoured kelp to fight off the disease. Not because of its purported health benefits, but because of its name. You see, in China, SARS was also called *Feidian*, a usage that began to quickly fade since the term is used for a whole family of cold or flu-like diseases, SARS being just one branch. Either way, *Feidian* is a word composed of two parts: "Fei," meaning "lack" or "no," and "dian," which can mean "kelp." So, some citizens put the words together, thinking that *Feidian* meant "no kelp." Hence, a belief sprung up that if a person ate lots of seaweed, it might result in "no SARS."

Granted, many educated people in Beijing didn't buy into these purported remedies, but most wished they could have suspended their skepticism just long enough to do so. Confidence is key in times like these. Instead, most people tried to prevent infection by more sensible means: washing their hands constantly, wearing masks, washing their hair, removing their clothes as soon as they got home, and taking herbal medicines recommended by Beijing physicians.

As the first real reports emerged from the government about SARS and Beijing on April 20th, and the citizens watched the number of SARS cases rise each day from sixty to eighty to usually over a hundred, the panic in the city became palpable. With fears of shortages, there was a run on food—instant noodles flew off store shelves; fifty-pound bags of rice were carted home.

On Beijing's damp and empty streets, the mood was gloomy. Suddenly every day felt drenched with rain, the kind where, if you did go out, you very well *could* catch your death of cold. Subways were thought extremely dangerous, because it was believed no natural cross-breeze existed to blow lingering SARS particles away. Later it was heard that three cases of SARS were linked to the same Beijing bus, so suddenly people were afraid to board *them* as well. As a result, those who could resorted to taxis, which were considered a much safer, more isolated mode of transport. At least this *was* the case, until it was figured out that SARS patients obviously couldn't take buses to the hospital, only taxis. Suddenly Beijingers had no place to turn.

Despite all this, some of my Chinese friends proved quite brave in the face of SARS.

Now, let me backtrack a little here, and say that whenever I travel, before heading to a new country I often will first contact locals there through sites like ICQ, Yahoo, and Hotmail, exchanging e-mails with them for a few months prior to my trip so that by the time I arrive in a land completely alien to me, I have built-in friends. It makes my first few weeks there much easier and, in a way, more like home. One of these Internet friendships I made was with a delightful Beijinger named Lucia [pronounced loo-see-ah] (her English name), who in her bio had noted she was a devout Communist, something which intrigued me in that I wanted to hear her views on the subject, and hear her views on my *own* country. Her parents had been teachers whom, during the Cultural Revolution, had quit their jobs to go work in the fields with the farmers like many other Communists. Lucia's boyfriend, however, who was also Chinese, did not share her government views, something which led to the majority of their arguments.

Somehow or other, interesting incidents always seemed to crop up whenever Lucia swung by my hotel to pick me up for some outing. The first time we met, we had planned to head to Beijing's famed Temple of Heaven, a favorite landmark of the old emperors. When she arrived, she informed me her parents wouldn't be joining us. I asked her why, but it took a while for the answer to come out, Lucia looking a bit embarrassed. After about ten minutes of persistence on my part, she finally explained. It seemed her parents thought *I* was a spy... A spy for George W. Bush.

Now, as unlikely as this might have been—and trust me, it is *really* unlikely—rumors, as I mentioned earlier, were running rampant in Beijing, and one such rumor was that *SARS* was a manmade creation, a joint effort by China's two most bedeviling foes: the U.S. and Taiwan. These two countries, according to Chinese rumor, had apparently co-leased some labs together in order to produce an epic undertaking of microscopic proportions. (For all I know, Biff himself probably started this rumor.)

As for my James Bond–like part in all this? I was supposed to be one of the carriers of the disease—a Typhoid Michael, if you will—who had been sent by the U.S. to spread the virus amongst the Chinese populace in order to accomplish two things: cripple the burgeoning Chinese economy and distract the world from America's much-criticized invasion of Iraq. This belief was backed up by reports that, up to that time, no recorded cases of SARS had appeared in the U.S., though we *had* apparently seen fit to infect our neighbor to the north. *Bye-bye, Toronto.*

It was at the beginning of this same outing, when Lucia picked me up at my hotel, that she remarked to me, "So where are you going to move to?"

I was a bit baffled. "Uh... *move* to?"

"You mean they didn't tell you?"

"They?"

"*Yes, they're closing down your hotel...* because of SARS."

"When?"

"Today."

"*What?!*"

Thankfully, I did eventually find a new hotel later that day. At least until they closed that one, too. In fact, this began a whole string of hotel closings underneath me, which further encouraged me to travel to southern China—*if I could get there.*

I say this because there was a fear at the time that none of us in Beijing would be allowed to leave the city without first undergoing a ten-day quarantine—where we'd end up in some bare white room, I suppose, while the authorities studied and poked at us. Detainment of this sort would definitely put a damper on my domestic travel plans in China.

Regarding my second hotel though, before it too closed down due to SARS—one day I was walking back to my new lodgings, when I saw a gaggle of reporters on the sidewalk before me, snapping pictures and toting TV cameras. At the center of the hubbub was a pop singing star, a sort of Chinese Roy Orbison in his 20s, with thick red-rimmed glasses and luminescent tennis shoes. He carried dozens and dozens of yellow roses, each individually wrapped, as many as his arms could hold.

Now, let me pause here and say that, in the past, I have been one to take advantage of opportunities where I can, often venturing into areas and situations where manners and ethics—and smarts—would often put off a brighter and more respectful fellow. Of course, me being curious as to what this was all about, I stopped to watch, and as the group moved from the curb in toward a massive building behind us, I noticed a young woman who was lugging a camera for the Japanese NHK network having trouble carrying all her equipment. Two men were with her, but they had apparently designated her the "muscle," despite her slight size, the two of them being content to carry really heavy notepads or microphones instead. So being a gentleman, but also recognizing an opportunity, I scrambled up to help her, catching a tripod just as it was headed for the cement.

So as the thick nut of reporters made their way into the mysterious building, I inserted myself into the crowd, tripod in hand, in my new role as part of the tech crew. We eventually reached an enormous elevator, and getting aboard, a few floors later we exited as one into an enormous room that resembled Mission Control at NASA, replete with enormous video screens and banks of computer consoles.

Official-looking officials greeted the singer as the press struggled to record it all. The singer began handing out his roses, one to each administrator, who smiled and thanked him, as they introduced him to the elaborate mega-tech features of the facility. Eventually, we were all led to another vast room, filled with rows and rows of desks and computers, each manned by a doctor or nurse. The sight pretty much confirmed my suspicions, for I knew as we progressed further the building was some sort of hospital. I just hadn't realized what *type* of hospital exactly… It seemed I had walked into the very nerve center of the whole fight against SARS in Beijing, the

SARS headquarters as it were. And me—as usual—with no mask.

Partly because of my naked face and partly because this was really someplace I should never have been, I made sure I stuck with the group, helping the camera girl if she needed it, but basically watching the little ceremonies as they unfolded. Though working for a Japanese network, the girl was actually Chinese, and explained that the singer had come to the hospital to hand out a rose to each of the workers braving the SARS environment and working so diligently to combat the crisis. The banks of phones and computers in the adjacent room were where they took calls from Beijingers and others across China reporting possible SARS cases or needing information and requesting help.

This nerve center was actually why my second hotel had to close its doors—to tourists anyway. We were essentially kicked out to make room for the busloads of doctors and nurses who were being brought in to Beijing to help. Since they would be working directly with SARS patients every day, it was considered unsafe for us to remain in the same hotel with them.

Which led to my third hotel in Beijing, and probably the nicest one. It was certainly the most posh of my accommodations so far, but it still came with its own peculiarities, thanks to the current crisis. For instance, every day, typically in the afternoon, there would be a knock on my hotel door. I'd open it to see a young man or woman, one of the hotel attendants, who would fail in their broken English to make clear exactly what they wanted before they raised a pistol-like device, pointed it at my forehead, and pressed the trigger. This "gun," shall we call it, was new on the scene in Beijing, and had been brought in to combat the spread of the disease. It was a thermometer gun, or "thermo-gun," if you will, which instantly gave its bearer a reading of your body temperature.

The hotel would check you every time you returned from some outing, even before you reached the front desk sometimes.

Now, despite all the hotel closings, I suppose one of the more interesting things was that most of Beijing's restaurants had remained open, creating quite unusual situations. For instance, when I would drop by some restaurant for lunch, even if it was a Kentucky Fried Chicken, the staff would be incredibly pleased to see me, mask or no mask, chiefly because I was their only patron that day. So I would have the entire restaurant to myself, sometimes with a wait staff of ten or fifteen people at my beck and call. As often as not, they would sit down at the table beside me and strike up conversation, being that they were incredibly bored. So every meal was a kind of meet and greet for me—and the Chinese were always so very kind to me anyway, this just made my dining all the more delightful.

Speaking of food, to my surprise, one day I ran into Biff again, back at my new hotel. From the look of his beard, he'd obviously visited a KFC recently, too. He arrived at my hotel about a half week after I had, being it was one of the only ones left open in Beijing, and as he'd exited the taxi and gone after his suitcase in the trunk, the hotel's attendant outside had come up and pointed one of those thermo-guns at good-old paranoid Biff's head.

The first thing that crossed my mind was how I could've possibly missed Biff's shriek from my hotel room only seven floors above the street.

Needless to say, he and his heart survived the incident, even if his tonsils half gave out.

Incidentally, I *was* able to later leave the city, in order to travel to other parts of China, a privilege the greater majority of Chinese did not have in that time of SARS—not without them first being quarantined for a week and a half. Such travel restrictions weren't put in place for internationals, perhaps because the Communist government feared any awkward incidents might anger outside business interests and thus further damage the Chinese economy. Of course, the possibility existed that the disease *could spread further* by giving internationals like us free reign, but they obviously felt it a risk worth taking.

Some Chinese citizens even had the entire areas where they lived essentially quarantined. For instance, one fellow I knew, who lived in a multi-building high-rise apartment complex in Beijing, could not come in or out of the perimeter without first passing by a makeshift guard shack, where security would check your ID to make sure you actually lived there. No one else was allowed to go in besides medical personnel and health inspectors because one of the latest SARS cases had come from my friend's apartment complex—in fact, from his very building. Worse yet, for all the tenants, the woman who'd become sick had worked in their building as the elevator operator, standing there all day long pushing the various floor buttons and breathing all over everything. All the tenants were terrified every day when they climbed into the elevator and the doors closed behind them. To combat possible infection, my friend always took a deep breath before climbing in, trying to hold it until he reached his apartment level. Problem was he lived on the twenty-sixth floor.

Even when I finally left Beijing to head south for Guilin by train, a twenty-four hour trip, I had my temperature taken by thermo-gun probably twenty times or more, a couple of times in the train station and what felt like every half hour by a special porter aboard the train.

As for me, I was eventually able to connect to the Internet to send my work back and forth to the U.S., simply by plugging into a local phone socket and dialing the Internet directly, no less, a service free in China. Feel free to insert your own suspicions here.

The reason why I never wore a mask while I was there? Well, despite the sometimes incredible danger involved at that time, I didn't really feel it was as perilous as many feared. For instance, during the SARS crisis, more people perished from regular flu in the U.S. alone than were lost to SARS worldwide. Mind you, these were not people who were in the flower of life who passed away, as those who contracted SARS often were, but still it was a sobering statistic to me. In fact, in a single week— again, in just the U.S.—more people perished in car accidents than died from SARS. To me, SARS was just another danger in life, an extra week of car wrecks. But a very sobering week, because it could have gotten very easily out of hand and run roughshod over the world the way the Spanish flu had done back in 1918, killing millions and millions across the globe. That's exactly what the World Health Organization was desperately trying to prevent.

However, despite the fear permeating everything back then in that truly Forbidden City, Beijingers eventually adapted—all the Chinese, in fact—often diffusing the threat with the greatest weapon of all, humor. Go to the airport and you'd be treated to a

SARS fashion show of designer surgical masks. Businesswomen in suits wore masks and gloves color-coordinated to match their ensembles. And though the prevailing fashion for masks was standard white, the masks of some men resembled army fatigues, or sported splashes of color that turned them into Jackson Pollock paintings. Many masks for the women bore small roses, peaches, or snowflakes stitched into their fronts. Other designs were even more playful, incorporating Winnie the Pooh, Mickey Mouse, and a certain Warner Bros. rabbit. One mask making the rounds was pink and shaped like a pig's snout, with two black dots on the front. Another even had that special Beijing kiss I mentioned earlier adorning its outsides—in bright red lipstick.

Meanwhile, SARS jokes abounded on the Internet. Song lyrics were transformed into comical odes supposedly penned by a lonely lovesick virus that longed to be near people, and wanted to *move in* with them. Even one of Chairman Mao's poems was humorously tailored for the times.

If there was one good thing to come out of the SARS crisis though, it was that families became closer. Being that so many people were off from work and bound to their lodgings, many Beijingers said they had come to treasure the extra time they were able to spend with their families—to visit with grandchildren they hadn't seen nearly enough, or sons who rarely had time between work weeks to stop by. Relationships with friends had grown deeper as well.

"I call my friends all the time now," one of my Chinese friends told me. "Everyone is so worried about SARS. The first thing we always say is a joke, *'Have you got it?'* There's more talk between strangers, too. It is rare for us. But now we talk to everyone. We ask taxi drivers if they are scared about SARS, and if their families are worried about them doing this job."

More than anything else, however, the people of Beijing had acclimated to the danger, and every day they went about their business a little more routinely, even if clad in mask and gloves. That masked kiss by the young couple in that famous photo I brought up earlier, the one so popular in China, though silly perhaps, it seemed to embody the mood and the people's reaction in a nutshell: No matter what would happen in Beijing, or all of China, all things would carry on—life, even *love*—in the time of SARS.

Michael McGee is an award-winning Northern California writer who's been lucky enough to travel the world to work with elephants in the jungles of Thailand and dance with Geishas in Kyoto. He's also the author of several fantasy/scifi works, including the critically-acclaimed novel *String of Pearls*, an epic thriller set in Heaven and Hell and recommended for a Hugo Award for Best Novel of the Year. In addition, he's penned two travel story collections, *The Great Big Bungalow – Volumes 1 & 2* and is co-winner of the Lowell Thomas Travel Book of the Year Award. To find out more about Michael, go to:

<u>www.michaelmcgeebooks.com</u>

ACKNOWLEDGMENTS

HorrorAddicts.net would like to thank all the authors, the artist, and the editor for making this book available and for donating their time to a worthy cause.

We would also like to thank the listeners, readers, and donators of HorrorAddicts.net for your continued support throughout the year.

Thank you for purchasing this book and doing your part to make disaster relief a reality.

HorrorAddicts.net

Do you love horror?
Want to hear a podcast created by
horror fanatics just like you?
Listen to HorrorAddicts.net.

Real horror reported by real horror fans.
We cover the news and reviews of horror:

☠movies ☠games ☠books
☠manga ☠anime ☠music
☠comics ☠locations ☠events
☠rpgs ☠fashion ☠more!

Every episode features horror authors, podcasters,
movie people, musicians, and horror personalities.

Featuring the annual Wicked Women Writers and
Masters of Macabre Challenges, the reality sitcom
GothHaus, 100 Word Stories, and music from
graveconcernsezine.com

Your one stop horror source:

HorrorAddicts.net

FROM HORRORADDICTS.NET

the wickeds

HorrorAddicts.net presents thirteen horror tales from up-and-coming women writers. This diverse collection of revenge, torture, and macabre is sure to quench any horror addict's thirst for blood. Between these covers reside werewolves, demons, ghosts, vampires, a voodoo priestess, headless horseman, Bloody Mary, and human monsters who are perhaps the most disturbing. All proceeds will be donated to LitWorld, a non-profit organization that uses the power of story to cultivate literacy leaders around the globe.

MORE BOOKS FROM CONTRIBUTING AUTHORS

Evil Reflection   by Larion Wills

David in the flesh was everything Sara could want, until he touched her and the horror of a past rape made her freeze. Only when he came to her in dreams could her body respond and welcome him. When the telegram came saying he was dead, she agonized over losing the one chance to break free of the mental blocks only for new terror to begin.

The Herd   by Ed Pope

Delve inside the mind of someone enslaved in a manner never before inflicted on human beings. Thought provoking and disturbing, The Herd is a vicarious journey to the limits of mental and physical suffering.

Undergrowth   by H. E. Roulo

Torsten is a xenobotanist whose specialization in dangerous plants has already meant death for someone he loved. The Lumentera plant's hallucinogenic and luminescent qualities make it an invaluable commodity. But when the Lumentera blooms, the bait is set in a mind game whose outcome is as uncertain as Torsten's sanity.

FlagShip Steampunk Special Issue   by Philip Carroll

Featuring "Boys Will Be Boys" by Philip Carroll. Turning lead into gold should have been a simple alchemical task, the boys thought. Dad just wasn't using enough phlogiston. Never mind the explosive side-effects...

Artistic License   by Emerian Rich

Imagine if everything you painted came alive. Leslie Marietta faces this reality when she inherits her family estate. Enchantment and wonder transform her life into a fairytale, but as with all fairytales, there is a dark presence. Phantom servants sneak through the house, horrifying shadow creatures threaten to destroy her, and a band of Edwardian house guests are trapped in the walls.

Ivory   by Steve Merrifield

Martin is a painter whose creativity is slipping away. One night he hits a woman with his car. The woman survives and has white hair and jet black eyes. Martin becomes obsessed with her and in order to be with her he now faces dangers of this world and another.

Traitor   by Mark Eller

Last Chance - a small town set on the edge of the far frontier. It is a place of gentle manners and common civility. Times change when a Talent Master runs rampant, savages threaten war, and an illegal militia from an alternate universe plans invasion. A hero is needed. A Savior. Meet Aaron Turner, the small unassuming man who runs the Last Chance General Store. He is this town's--this world's--only hope.

Mad Shadows   by Garth von Buchholz

A second edition collection of dark poetry by author Garth von Buchholz. It includes the title poem, Mad Shadows, as well as 12 other works that were previously published in magazines and journals. For more information visit the author's official website: vonBuchholz.com

Red Dreams   by Chris Ringler

Here are fifteen tales that will remind you why you fear the darkness and the night. Here are the children of broken hearts and shattered hopes.

Lilith's Love   by Dan Shaurette

When vampire hunters find them in New Orleans, Lilith and her friend Anna flee to where they think no one would expect to find vampires: The Valley of the Sun, Phoenix, Arizona, where they meet Donovan and Christian. As two romances are sparked, they must fight the vengeful plans of Lilith's Master.

Imaginariun 2012   by Timothy Reynolds

Featuring "Hawkwood's Folly" by Tim Reynolds. From the streets of Paris to the sea floor off the coast of North Africa, "Hawkwood's Folly" draws an English lord, a French doctor, and a young Russian bo's'n's mate into the deadly ocean depths on their quest to build a Utopia where no man has ventured before.

Heroes Arise   by Laurel Anne Hill

In a world where justice is achieved through careful customs of vengeance, a noble being pursues love and the preservation of his honor. Yet can he learn to reach into his own personal darkness and find the inner peace he craves?

Wicked Initiations   by Jennifer Rahn

Vladdir, King of the Temlochti State, must fight against an inherited curse that fills him with cannibalistic desires. There is only one way out – to set free the Pure Continuance of the King who roamed the Desert before him.

The Great Big Bungalow   by Michael McGee

A collection of unusual travel tales and beautiful photos from across the globe. Includes stories about dancing with Geishas in Japan, working with elephants in the jungles of Thailand, living with the Bedouin in the deserts of Arabia, and many more. Several stories are humorous, recalling the writings of travel sage, Bill Bryson.

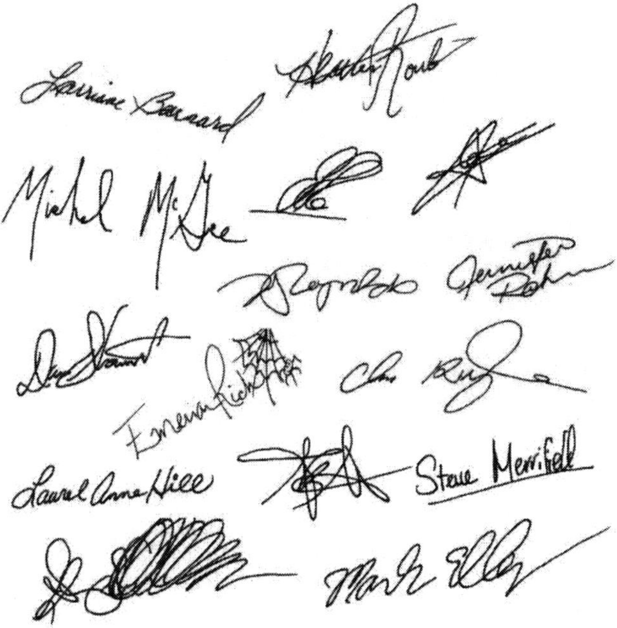
Laurel Anne Hill
Steve Merrifield

Since 1988, Rescue Task Force has been alleviating suffering and bringing support, relief, and love to disaster victims.

Arriving in a disaster area, the initial response team provides immediate assistance such as local purchasing and convoys relief supplies into hazardous zones. RTF teams typically work in remote, difficult to access isolated villages and hamlets that are overlooked by conventional relief providers.

Rescue Task Force goes where others do not, doing what others will not. From the jungles of Central America to the mountains of Kosovo, from tsunami ravaged Thailand and Sri Lanka and the interior of Afghanistan to hurricane and fire disaster stricken communities in the United States, RTF is there.

Rescue Task Force
Brings hope.
Around the world.
Around the clock.

www.rescuetaskforce.org